A Famous Kind of Love

Love in Sunrise Series Book 2

Loran Adelle Davis

L.A. DAVIS BOOKS

A Famous Kind of Love
© 2021 Loran Adelle Davis
LA Davis Books

Editor: Bethany Hendrix
Cover: Alistair Cameron
Logo and Designs: Alistair Cameron
Images from: Stock Photo Secrets

First Edition: October 26, 2021

Check out my website and sign up for my newsletter for updates!

Description

London

From the outside, my life looks perfect – great son, amazing job, and a smile permanently plastered to my face, but they don't know what goes on deep inside. Am I a tortured soul? Not even close, but I'm far from perfect. I haven't had my shit together ever, especially not when it comes to men.

That's why when the hottest bachelor in the nation walks into my hotel, I know I have to ignore the instant attraction between us for two reasons – 1. I don't date guests. 2. He's so far out of my league.

Too bad, my body and my heart don't agree with my mind. I know this is a disaster waiting to happen, but how can I say no to the literal man of my dreams?

Jamie

I'm mesed up. That's all there is to it.

My life was perfect until that night when I destroyed a family's life. Now, I don't even recognize the face I see in the mirror. I'm just a shell of the man I once was, but then she walks into my life.

Her bright smile does something to me I can't explain. I can't stay away no matter how hard I try, but I have to, I made a pact with myself that I can't break.

Then, I see her face again, and I don't give a shit. I need her like I need every breath I take.

Contents

To my mama,
The one and only person who's had my back from birth. I love your kind spirit and ever-present love. You're truly the strongest person I know.

One

London

I hate my job. It's as simple as that. I hate that I'm the only one who ever seems to actually work. I hate that I can't have a day off without being called in to fix an issue. And I really hate the damn paperwork.

I shuffle the papers on my desk, trying to make sense of the mess the night manager left for me. Invoices, check-in forms, and random post-its are scattered all over. You'd think the title *Manager* on the door and my name underneath would keep people from venturing in when I'm gone, but clearly not. It doesn't matter that there's a designated spot for these papers in the main office.

I sort the papers out into piles, making the mess feel slightly more organized. Huffing out a breath, I place the last paper on its designated pile. This mess might look more organized, but it's still not where it's supposed to be.

I lean my elbows on the desk in front of me and rub my temples. You'd think after working at the Grand Sun Hotel for almost a decade I'd be used to this disaster, but I'm not. The owner, Brent, refuses to let me handle the hiring or, well, anything really. Yet, he's never actually around, and he's always calling me to fix his messes.

If he'd let me handle things in the first place, this chaotic mess of a business would run a lot smoother.

It's not like I didn't grow up in this hotel. My mom worked here all through my childhood. Hell, some days it felt like she lived here. She worked so much when I was growing up that I rarely ever saw her. A part of me believes she did that on purpose. Even when she wasn't working, she didn't spend her free time with me. I was left to my own devices from a very early age.

That's a major difference between my mom and me. I spend every free moment with my eight-year-old son, even if they are few and far between at times. He is and always will be my priority.

A soft knock on the door frame stops me in my tracks. I look up to see Lilah, the front desk assistant, staring at me. She doesn't say anything, almost like she's waiting for me to speak first.

"Can I help you?" I say, slightly annoyed.

She nods her head. "There's a man that wants a room, but he looks a little sketchy. He's wearing dark sunglasses and a baseball hat."

"Okay, but we don't turn away people because of how they look. Get him a room."

Her face twists in disgust. "But he freaks me out. Can you just come out and take care of him?" she whines.

I can't tell if she's really freaked out or if she's just trying to get out of doing her job. Knowing Lilah, it's the latter. I think I've only seen her do her job a handful of times, but I'm not allowed to fire her because she's the boss' niece.

I drop the papers I'm holding onto my desk and stand, sighing. I want to make a smart-ass remark about how every customer must freak her out, but I keep my mouth shut.

"Fine, I'll take care of it," I pause, studying her reaction. She grins, her eyes shining with mischief. "But you can go to the storage room and unpack the shipment that came in today."

Her grin falls into a frown, and she rolls her eyes, stomping her foot like the bratty teenager she is, but she doesn't argue with me.

I make my way around my desk and down the hall in the opposite direction of Lilah. I reach the front counter in less time than usual. "Hello," I greet the customer, his back to me and his nose in his phone.

He must not hear me because he doesn't move.

I take in his full frame, broad shoulders, and amazing butt. His muscles are so defined that I can see their creases through the tight, black shirt. His baseball cap covers his longer, dark hair, but not so much that I can't see a few specks of gray here and there.

Instantly, I feel things in places I shouldn't, especially not about a guest. It doesn't matter that I can't see his face, I can already tell he's a gorgeous man.

I clear my throat, reminding myself I have a job to do, and it isn't checking out this unbelievably large man in front of me. "Excuse me, sir, can I help you?" I say a little louder this time.

He jumps and swivels around on his heels. "Yes, I need to..." he pauses, his gaze landing on mine. I can't see his eyes behind the sunglasses, but I imagine he's feeling the same things coursing through my own body.

Slowly, he slips his glasses off, and our eyes meet. There's something in his brown eyes that makes it nearly impossible for me to breathe. He's not just gorgeous. His features are almost god-like; not a wrinkle creases his face as his lips twist up into a confident smile.

I know him, I think as I study his face. Then, it hits me. The world's hottest bachelor is standing in front of me. He's not just hot, he's also one of the top action movie stars in Hollywood, and my son's idol.

I try not to swoon, forcing my inner fan girl to shut up. I hide all recognition of who he is and pretend I don't know him at all.

That's the easy part though. What's not easy is ignoring the heat rising to my cheeks while his stare burns my skin.

He shakes his head slightly and speaks, "I need a room."

"Well you've come to the right place," I say, smiling. "Do you have any special requests for your room?"

10

He shakes his head again, this time more defined. "Just that it's comfortable and available for the next few months," he answers, glancing at his phone as it buzzes from its spot in his hand.

I don't miss the "few months" part, and I'm curious as to why he'll be staying here that long. There are no movies being filmed anywhere near here of which I'm aware. But it's none of my business, and he's not the first celebrity to grace our hotel.

The beauty of a small town like Sunrise is people can come here to hide out and relax. We may be a gossipy lot at times, but we know when to keep our noses out of it. Not to mention, most of the people here don't care about anyone outside this town.

Once Skylar Clark, the number one actress in America, came to stay for a month after a brutal scandal involving her and a married man hit the headlines. Not a single person in town even realized who she was until after she'd already left. It just so happened that old Mable from the grocery store got bored behind the counter one day and decided to read the gossip rags.

I love this town, but we are still behind the times. Things like that don't intrigue us, but that's not the point.

No, the point is Jamie Decker just happens to be the hottest celebrity to ever grace our small corner of the world. That's all. No big deal.

If only my body could catch up to my head.

"I'm sure we can find you a room to call home for a while," I tell him with a sweet smile.

He smiles back. "Also, discretion would be great as well. I'd prefer no one know I'm here," he whispers to me, acting like I know who he is.

"Of course, we always adhere to the strongest standards of discretion, Mr. Um, what's your name?" I ask, wanting to laugh at my poor attempt at acting.

He quirks a skeptical brow. "You don't know who I am?"

I hate lying. I really do, but one of the things our hotel is known for is our blatant lack of bothering the wealthier customers that stay here.

"No, I don't believe I do. Have you stayed here before?"

He blows out a sigh of relief that confuses me a bit. I can't tell if he's relieved that I don't know who he is, or he's figured out I'm a total liar and he's glad I'm pretending. The hint of a smile at the corner of his lips suggests it could be either. "A long time ago, but I'm sure you weren't working here then," he says.

"Probably not," I smile. I would have remembered him staying here if I'd been working here then.

I tap some keys on the computer and pull up our reservation program. It's almost the end of summer, which makes finding a room for an extended time difficult, but I rearrange the reservation schedule a bit, making it possible to accommodate his request.

"Okay, we have a room available on the 2nd floor. Will that work for you?" I ask, sneaking a peek at him above the computer screen. My insides twist with warm and fuzzies.

He nods. "That would be great."

"Great, can I get the name for the reservation and your ID, please?"

He reaches in his back pocket and fishes out his wallet. "Jamie Decker," he states, handing me his ID.

When I grab the ID from his hand, our fingers brush lightly together, and I feel it - that spark that people talk about when they meet someone. It rushes through my body and straight to my core. Even if it's a simple attraction or a burning chemistry, it's not something I've had the pleasure of feeling before, not like this anyway. Somehow, I just know I'll never be the same after this.

I brush it off, reminding myself he's a customer, but it doesn't keep my heart or my stomach from doing crazy flips.

I check his ID, confirming that he is the one-and-only Jameson Decker, action movie star, activist, and hottest bachelor in the nation. For a moment, I think I might faint, but I mentally slap myself back into reality.

It doesn't matter how hot he is, I cannot swoon over him for two very large reasons: 1. He's a guest, and 2. He is so far out of my league, like I'm not even sure we're both on the same planet.

I hand his ID back to him. "Thank you, Mr. Decker. I have your room assigned for you." I pick up a key card, scan it, and lay it on the counter in front of him. "Here's your room key. You'll be in room 206. Our cleaning staff comes once a day, but if you'd like, I can make a note to come less since you'll be staying longer."

"That would be perfect. Once or twice a week should be fine," he says, taking the key card and slipping it in his pocket.

"I'll make a note for you. Do you need me to show you your room?" I ask, desperately hoping I can make this moment last a little longer.

He shakes his head. "I think I can find it."

"Perfect. If you need anything, please don't hesitate to ask me." I pick up my business card and hand it to him. "There's my personal number. Just call or text, and we'll get you what you need."

And you can text or call me any damn time for any reason.

He rubs his thumb across my name on the business card and grins. "Thank you, London. I'll see you around." He turns to leave, and I slink against the wall beside me.

Did I really just do that - give my personal number to a movie star? I must be completely insane to think he'd ever use it.

I shake my head and push off the wall, walking back to my office. I've lost my mind.

Taking a seat at my desk, I slip out my phone and pull up Google, typing his name in the search tab. Numerous photos pop up on the screen. Most of them include him and some girl - some totally thin, model type, gorgeous girl. I can't help but compare my thicker hips to her and feel disgusted.

I click out of the pictures and scroll through some articles. Some question if he's getting back together with his ex while others talk about an accident that happened a couple months ago. I had no idea he'd been in an accident. Clearly, I don't pay much attention to the world outside Sunrise.

A nagging desire to read the articles hits, and my finger wavers over the link. The brief description doesn't give me much detail as to what happened, but I vaguely remember rumors about a family and someone dying. I didn't believe most of it, and I didn't realize he was the actor involved. I know how most of the stuff printed in those tabloids aren't what really happened. Not to mention, I don't read them anyway.

I resist the urge to read the gossip rags and close out the search engine. None of it matters.

Except that's a complete lie; it matters to me. I'm curious about this man who chose to hide out in nowhere South Carolina and who gave me the kind of electric shocks I've never felt around a man before.

Even though he didn't say he's hiding out, I know that's what he's doing. What person in their right mind with that kind of money would choose to spend their time here unless they're hiding out?

Okay, a lot of people do, but they don't normally have his status.

I open Google again, wanting to quench my curiosity and close it just as fast. No matter how badly I want to know what they say, it's not my business. He's just a guest. And I'm just a broke ass, single mom who spends every waking minute working.

Well, maybe not every minute, but it damn sure feels like it.

A Famous Kind of Love

Two

Jamie

For some reason, even hours later, I can't get her out of my mind. That pretty little thing that walked up to the counter, pretended like she didn't know me, and gave me a spot to lay low for a while is forever ingrained in my brain. Even if nothing can happen between us, I let my mind wonder to thoughts of touching her and those sexy curves.

She's much fuller in the hips than my previous girlfriends, but I like that so much better.

And that spark. I know she felt it, too. I saw it in her eyes. I never believed in that shit, but now, I think I do. For a minute, I thought I'd lost my mind when I felt that shock race through me. I've always thought that shit only happened in those stupid romance movies, but I know better now. That feeling was real.

Too bad it doesn't matter. None of it does.

I force myself away from thoughts of - what was her name? London? Instead, I focus on the reason I'm here in the first place.

I pull the internet tab up on my phone and go to the saved pages. I hit the first page that pops up and scroll through the articles until I find what I'm looking for. I don't know why I torture myself this way every day, but it's become a habit.

I need to do it to remind myself of what I used to be - a king of Hollywood. I ruled the action movie scene. I always had a girl on my arm and an award-winning smile plastered to my face. My name was in every tabloid, just like it is now, but for very different reasons.

I tap on the article, waiting for it to load. "Famous Celebrity Involved in Deadly Car Crash: New Information," flashes across the screen. It doesn't matter how many months have passed since the incident; the press just won't leave it alone.

I read the article, reliving the night I'll never forget.

It's black and rainy. The roads are slick. I'm not driving fast like usual, instead I'm trying to be careful. I've seen too many accidents happen on this road at night. Except it doesn't matter. I'm being too cautious, and I miss the animal that runs out into the road. It happens so fast. I swerve at the last minute, not seeing the car coming straight at me.

Before I can hit the brakes, our cars collide into each other, jolting me forward into blackness.

I shudder at the memory of the impact. It was an accident, but that didn't matter to the family who lost their child or to the press. They've turned it into prime-time news.

I click out of the article and lean my head back against the chair in my large hotel room. I close my eyes and all I see are flashing lights around me, emergency personnel running back and forth.

I was lucky. At least, that's what the doctors kept saying. I had some bruises, lacerations, a couple of broken ribs, and a concussion, but I was alive. Strangers reminded me of that every day - not only in the hospital, but in the tabloids as well.

I take several deep breaths, trying my best to ground myself back into reality and calm my beating heart. If I could go back, I would, but I know there's nothing I could have done differently.

That's why I'm here - to get away from it all and try to forget the best I can. Only I don't want to forget it all. I feel too damn guilty.

A buzzing from my phone pulls me from my pity party. I don't look at the name on the screen. I just pick up the phone and answer robotically.

Damon, my manager and only real friend in Hollywood, answers, "Damn, Jamie, you sound like shit."

"Gee, thanks," I respond with the little energy left in me. Reliving that moment always seems to drain me.

"Just calling it like I hear it," he laughs, trying to lighten the mood. It doesn't work. Nothing could make me crack a smile at the moment.

I grunt my response and rub my temples, easing the tension that's built up in my head and shoulders.

"Did you make it to Sunrise okay?" he asks, his voice softening a bit. He's always been more my friend than my manager, something you don't find often in this industry. Of course, it probably helps that we've known each other longer than our working relationship.

"Yea, I did. I got a room at the hotel here."

"Good, and you trust they can be discreet about your stay?" he asks, always concerned about my welfare.

"Yea, it's one of those small coastal towns with lots of wealthy tourists. I have no doubt they won't notice me at all. And if they do, I doubt they'll say anything," I assure him.

"I'll send over an NDA just to be safe," he says, unconvinced.

"I don't think it's necessary, but whatever you think."

"I think it's better to be safe than sorry," he sighs, and instantly, I picture him pinching the bridge of his nose. "I don't want you to spend the whole time there dwelling on what happened. Get out, see the town, and maybe even meet a nice girl. Decide what you want now after everything. And please don't use the accident as an excuse to not live anymore."

"I'll try," I say, not wanting to make any promises I can't keep, which is exactly what I'd be doing.

The accident screwed me up in ways I can't even begin to explain. The guilt eats at me every day, making me wish it had been me who'd died instead of that little girl. How do I begin to live with something like that? How do I go back to the life I had before?

I don't think I can. Everything about this situation has changed me, and I know I won't ever be the same.

"Have you thought anymore about what we discussed?" Damon asks on the end of a sigh.

"Yea," I answer mechanically. Of course, I've thought about it, but talking to some judgmental stranger about what happened just doesn't seem very appealing to me.

"I really think you need to see a counselor. It would do you so much good to talk and work through all your emotions. You'll never be able to move past all this if you don't face it," he insists.

"So you keep saying," I grumble. Damon's been trying to get me to see a counselor for a couple months now. He genuinely thinks it will help, but I think they're all quacks. I know he means well, and maybe there's something to what he's saying. I'm just not sure talking to a stranger is what I need.

"Look, at least consider it. Find someone in the area and give it a try. Might surprise you."

"I'll look, but I'm not making any promises," I respond, promptly ending the call with a hurried goodbye.

I don't want to talk anymore, especially not to the one person who knows where I am and why.

I toss my phone on the coffee table, crossing my arms in front of me as I let the cushions of the chair swallow me up.

I will try. I'll really try to make the most of this time away from my new reality.

I shut my eyes and drown out the world around me, focusing on the soft sounds of the waves outside my window and the comforting feel of the chair around me. There's one light on, illuminating the small living area just opposite the bed. My feet are propped up on the rectangular wooden coffee table and to my left is a large couch.

I like the set-up of the room. I even enjoy the old wing-backed chair that sits between the bed and the wall-length window. The mid-afternoon sun barely peeks through the darkening curtains hanging tightly closed.

I don't know how long I sit there when a soft knock sounds on my door. I push myself out of the chair, feeling slightly annoyed. I thought I told them I didn't want service every day.

I look through the peep hole and see a familiar face. Her cheeks are flushed, and she's wringing her hands with what I assume are nerves.

She looks so damn cute and sexy, the way she stands there, almost shaking with nerves. It's something I'm not used to at all - women intimidated by me. No, I'm used to women throwing themselves at me with a lust-filled confidence.

I chuckle softly and don't miss the way she affects me,

making me almost giddy with excitement and a need I can't quite explain. I feel like a teenage boy again about to embark on his first journey with a girl. I don't know why I feel this way around her, but I'd guess it has to do with how different she appears than what I'm used to.

As much as I want to run from this feeling, it's also the first time in months I've felt any sort of emotion other than numb.

I open the door, figuring I've made her wait long enough. She's about to walk away when she hears the door squeak open.

"Hey there," I say, not having to force the smile I'm wearing.

"Hey," she mutters, her cheeks darkening a deeper shade of red. "I'm sorry to bother you. I'm just on my way out for the day and wanted to make sure you have everything you need."

I'm flattered that she thought of me and a little skeptical, too. I've had way too many women do nice things for me just to get in my bed, and I don't need or want that.

But I don't get that vibe from her. Her ocean blue eyes are full of genuine sparkle and her soft features tell a story of innocence rather than deception.

"Thank you, but I think I'm good." My stomach grumbles at that exact moment, reminding me I haven't eaten all day.

She laughs. "I think your stomach might disagree."

"Yea, you might be right. Do you know of any places I can order some food?"

"The diner in town has amazing burgers, and there's a

restaurant downstairs. The food is great, and the alcohol is the good stuff. Other than that, there are a couple bars in town, with typical bar food."

I have no intentions of leaving this hotel tonight, so that makes my decision ten times easier. *Too bad, a certain, sexy woman won't be joining me.*

Stop, I tell myself. *Don't go there. You can't offer her anything, remember? You're simply a shell of the man you used to be.*

I do remember, far more vividly than I'd like too. I can't offer her anything other than a good time and I'm not sure she'd be down for that.

I let my eyes run over her body again, landing on her cherry red lips. The desire to taste her lips is far stronger than it should be, and I have no idea what to think about that. But, for the first time in a while, something other than the accident is occupying my mind.

Three

London

Okay, I'm definitely fangirling.

I mean, I went to his room to see if he needed anything before I left for the night. I never do that, like ever. It's against the rules I created for myself to avoid getting close to the guests.

I did it anyway. I knocked on his door and embarrassed the hell out of myself.

At least I got an even better look at his unbelievably handsome features. He'd ditched the baseball cap and was wearing sweats and a generic black T shirt. His jaw line was rough with stubble and his shaggy hair was styled just right.

I won't even get started on his eyes; something about the specks of gold mixed in with greens and browns captured my attention. Or maybe it was the megawatt smile and muscles that did it? Nope, it was definitely the eyes, even though they looked a little lost and confused. I just knew they held so many secrets, and I wanted to know them all.

I shake off all thoughts of Jamie as I swing open the door to my best friend's cafe. Loud voices assault me as I enter the busy space. I don't attempt to get in the line that's nearly out the door. Instead, I make my way through the mass of customers into the back where I find Ki sitting on a stool baking.

"Hey," I holler over the sound of the mixer.

She looks up at me and smiles, shutting the mixer off. "That's better," she says, standing and coming to give me a hug. "How are you?"

"I'm good." I say, squeezing her tight. "I see y'all are busy today. You might need to think about hiring some help."

She steps back and laughs. "Hunter keeps saying the same thing, especially with the baby coming."

"I mean, it's a good idea."

She nods, frowning. "I know. I just hate it. Besides, it's always been just Sabrina and Mario working with me here. What if hiring someone else changes the dynamic?"

"Yeah, but you being on maternity leave will change the dynamic anyway. At least, they'll have some extra hands until you get back," I reason.

Ki pouts and crosses her arms. "Why do you and Hunter always have to be so logical?" she whines.

I chuckle softly. "If we aren't, who else will be when it comes to your stubborn butt?"

"Okay, point taken," she says, rubbing her belly.

She's gotten bigger over the last few weeks. Her belly shows a little bit more each day under her larger T shirts. If I did the math correctly, I'd say she's about four or five months along by now.

I'll never forget the day we bought her the pregnancy tests to confirm our suspicions. I didn't entirely agree with Sabrina's assessment, but I knew she needed to make sure.

"So," Ki starts, "what brings you back to the kitchen today?"

"Nice change of subject," I say sarcastically, rolling my eyes.

Ki laughs. "You know I hate talking about me."

"No, you hate talking about things when you know the other person is right."

"Whatever," she mutters.

I take a deep breath. "I met someone yesterday," I say, a blush creeping to my cheeks.

Ki's eyes widen and she gasps. "Wait, what?"

I've had my fair share of men over the years, but they never pan out to be more than a warm body to keep me company. This one has potential, and not just because he's famous and hot as hell.

I can't quite explain why I believe this. I don't know much

about him, but standing at his hotel door last night and studying his face, I felt like I could see into some deep crevice of his soul. He looked forlorn and troubled, but his eyes also held a hint of something akin to excitement, like a dim light shining in the midst of a dark tunnel.

Call me crazy, but that moment told me more about him than any tabloid article could.

"I know. I think he's different."

"Uh huh, you mean unlike every other guy you always seem to find something wrong with after the first date?" Ki asks, skeptically.

She does have a point. I do always find something wrong with them after the first date, but it's not my fault they hide these weird quirks.

"Yes," I argue. "I mean, for one, he's crazy sexy, like defined muscles, strong jaws, unbelievable eyes sexy."

"I like where this is going. So, hotter than computer guy from Charleston?"

"A gazillion times hotter than him," I confirm.

Ki smirks. "He was the best looking one you've dated so far too."

I can't argue with that. I've dated some pretty interesting men, but it's hard to find decent guys in such a small town. I've probably dated half of them already, and not because I get around a lot, but because there just aren't that many men our age around here.

"So, what else can you tell me about this guy?" Ki prods, nodding in my direction.

"He seems really nice."

"Nice?"

"Yea," I say, cringing at how awful that word sounds when she says it. "There was this spark between us when our hands accidentally touched."

Just thinking about that spark sends shivers down my spine. That's the real reason I know he's different. I've never felt that spark with anyone, no matter how attractive I found them. I thought that instant attraction didn't exist. Maybe it's only some kind of sexual chemistry, but even if that's all it is, it's more than I've felt with any other guy. I feel like that says something about him.

"Oh, sparks are a good sign," Ki states, raising her eyes suggestively at me.

"Yeah, but he's so out of my league."

Ki rolls her eyes and huffs out a sigh. "I knew there was going to be a 'but'."

"Honestly, there's absolutely nothing wrong with him that I can tell, except…" I pause. My heart pounds as his name sits on the tip of my tongue. I want to tell Ki, but I made an agreement.

"Except?" she prods, holding on to my every word.

"I'm not supposed to say anything."

"No, you can't do that to me," Ki shrieks. "Come on, just tell me. You know I won't say anything."

I do know that, but it doesn't change the facts that I can't say a word. I shake my head firmly. "I can't. I signed an NDA, a legal document stating that I couldn't talk to anyone."

She gasps loudly, covering her mouth with her hand. "It's a celebrity, isn't it?" She points her forefinger at me, staring at me sneakily. "I bet it's that Jameson guy. You know the one in all the movies? I heard he's being sued for some accident he was in a while back. He's probably hiding out from all the press."

Shit, how could she possibly know that? My eyes widen slowly. I try to remain calm and force my face to stay neutral, but I know I'm about to give it all away. I've never been any good at lying no matter how hard I tried.

"Oh my goodness, it is him," she says, her eyes nearly popping out of her head.

I nod. "Yes, he came into the hotel looking for a room. I recognized him immediately thanks to Brayden's obsession with him."

"Please tell me you didn't fan girl on him."

"I didn't, surprisingly, but I did stop by his room on the way out last night to make sure he had everything he needed." My cheeks heat from my admission. I still feel so idiotic for doing that. I'd never do that for any other guest, but he's not just any other guest.

"Oh, London, look at you, going for what you want," Ki squeals.

"I don't know if I'd call it going for what I want. I mean I don't stand a chance with him. Plus, I don't date guests." I know I sound more like I'm trying to convince myself than Ki.

"Stop all of that. When was the last time you went for something you really wanted? And computer guy doesn't count since he asked you out first."

I cringe as I realize that I've never really gone after what I want. I've had the same job since high school. I've lived in the same town my whole life. And the guys have always asked me out.

"Never," I finally admit.

"You've just made my point. You need to do something for *you*. Forget all the things holding you back. If you want this man, go for it, especially if you think things could be different."

"So you think I should pursue him?" I ask, twisting on my feet.

I'm pretty sure all this happiness between Ki and Hunter has made her lose her damn mind. Besides, Jamie's probably immune to women chasing after him. I'm sure it happens all the time.

"I think you should do your best to make sure you come in contact with him as much as possible. Then, you should go for it," she insists, giving me a *what can it hurt?* look.

I laugh, slightly hysterical. "I've never done anything like that, and I have no clue how to even do it."

"Yes, you do. I mean you already have."

What does she mean I already have? I don't even get a chance to ask before Sabrina pops her head into the kitchen.

"Seriously, you didn't invite me to the party. I see how it is," she says, pouting.

"Sorry, you were busy," Ki says, shrugging her shoulders.

"Yea, yea," Sabrina chimes before sauntering up to us. "So, what did I miss?"

Ki begins to speak, and my cheeks heat before she even says a word. "London's got herself a new man."

"I do not," I huff, crossing my arms in front of me.

Ki eyes me with a sassy pout on her lips. "Hm, then what would you call him?"

"A guest at the hotel," I say firmly.

Sabrina winks in my direction. "So that's what we're calling them now?"

I drop my hands to my side and roll my eyes, knowing this isn't going to end unless I end it. "Gee, uh, I think I need to go get Brayden." I glance down at the watch on my wrist that ran out of battery a while back. "Yep, definitely need to go pick him up," I confirm, turning on my heels and heading towards the door leading out to the cafe.

"Liar," Sabrina yells from behind. "That watch has been broken since last Christmas."

I ignore her comment, picking up my pace. Sometimes, having close friends is a pain in my rear.

Four

Jamie

Nothing about my life over the last few months has been easy. Ever since that dreadful night, guilt has filled my soul. Even now, as I sit here on the couch in my room with my feet propped up on the coffee table and the TV playing some old comedy show, the memories of the incident fill my mind.

I know Damon is right. I know I need to get out and live my life, try to forget the best I can, but it's not that simple or that easy.

I've had enough tragedy in my life. I lost my parents at a young age. I dealt with the trauma, but I felt every emotion it brought me. Some days, it had been so strong I could barely breathe. Other days, I was lucky to push through it.

My grandma always told me I'd never make it in Hollywood because I had a heart. I cared too damn much, felt too damn hard. I brushed her off back then, thinking she was simply being dramatic, but once I made my way to the big city, I realized she wasn't all that wrong.

And that's why moving on from this is so hard for me. I do have a heart - a beating heart that feels every single emotion to the depth of its core. It won't let me forget what I did, even if it wasn't on purpose. It won't let me move on because I know I hurt more than just that girl. I hurt her entire family. I took their whole life away from them.

How am I supposed to move on from that - *forget* that?

My phone pings on the couch cushion beside me and I glance over to see who it is. Not that it could be many people. I don't give my personal number out for a reason.

Damon: Get out of your room. Get out of your head. And send me a damn picture so I know you actually did it.

Leave it to Damon to know I'd still be sitting in my room four days after my arrival.

I don't bother typing out a response, knowing it won't matter anyway. He won't listen to anything I say, not until I send him the fucking picture of the outdoors.

I slip my socked feet off the coffee table and stand, stretching as I do. There's a large imprint of my body on the couch cushion I've made my home since I arrived.

I should be ashamed, but I'm not. I've spent my whole adult life working my ass off to make something of myself. Then, when I finally did it, I just kept working. I think I deserve this little break, even if it's for a whole different reason than relaxing.

I slip on a pair of sneakers and head out the door of my room. I don't know where I'm going yet, but I do know it will be some place where I can avoid people as much as possible. Not only do I hope to avoid being recognized, but I don't want to socialize at all if possible.

At least, that's what I think until my eyes land on the fucking gorgeous hotel manager standing behind the front desk. She's flashed in and out of my thoughts often over the last few days, but she hasn't been able to dominate the horrific memories no matter how much I wish she could.

The guest she's helping - an older man with white hair - takes the key from her hand and says thank you before walking away shakily.

"Hey you," she greets, a warm smile covering her face and making her eyes crinkle at the sides.

Her smile nearly guts me with its warmth, but I welcome it. It's such a foreign feeling for me - one I haven't let myself feel in ages.

"Hey," I say, walking over to the counter where she stands.

"Haven't seen you in a few days. Thought I was gonna have to send a search and rescue team into your room." Amusement dances in her eyes.

"Would you have been part of that team?" I ask, shocking myself with my own flirting. I don't even remember the last time I hit on a woman, let alone said anything remotely flirty to them.

A coy smile plays on her lips. "Well, Mr. Decker, aren't you the big flirt today?" I can't deny the way hearing my name on her lips affects me.

"I'm just as shocked as you are," I admit with a somewhat tortured laugh.

"Aha, why do I feel like you're just saying that?"

"I'm not. I swear. It's not something I normally do often, especially not these days," I balk at the admission. Did I really just say that? Shit, I'm not sure I'm ready for this.

She shakes her head, chuckling. "If you say so," she drawls out. "So, what can I do for you today?"

I exhale a breath. Thank God, she changed the subject. I don't know if she's telepathic or could read the uncomfortable feeling on my face, but whatever it was, I'm glad she did it.

"Actually, I was wondering if you could tell me where the best places are to go and not be seen by a lot of people." That's not exactly why I came over here, but it'll do for now. Besides, it's the best excuse I have. I'm not sure saying I came over here to talk to the beautiful woman whom I can't seem to stop thinking about is the best option.

She puts her finger to her chin and taps lightly. "Hm, it's a little early for a bar, and the cafe would be fairly packed this morning," she says, thinking out loud. I rather enjoy listening to her debate the best places for me to go on a Thursday morning. "Are you looking for food or fresh air?"

Good question, I think as my stomach growls quietly. "Maybe a bit of both?"

"In that case, I'd say your best bet is to take a walk on the beach, then go over to the hotel restaurant for brunch. Our beach front is private, so there shouldn't be a lot of tourists out there unless they're staying here, and the restaurant is always quiet this time of day. Honestly, though, you could probably go anywhere in this town and no one would say a damn thing to you," she explains in the most matter of fact way.

"I see." I nod my head slowly, processing what she's saying. I know she knows who I am now. After all, she saw my license and Damon said something about sending an NDA over, both of which would give me away.

"Yea," she says, that same smile still glued to her face.

"You think you might want to go out for drinks this evening?" I blurt. I snap my lips together tightly, regretting the words instantly. Where the hell did they come from anyway?

She tilts her head to the side, looking perplexed and amused at the same time. "I'd love to," she says hesitantly while she studies my face.

I wonder if her hesitancy stems from the fact that my face looks like I just ate something sour. I'm sure she thinks I regret asking her that question or that I didn't really mean it. One of those would be right, but not for the reasons she'd think.

I only regret it because I haven't gone out on a date since before the accident. It goes against everything I promised myself the day I hurt that family. I figured if they couldn't have a happy, normal life, then neither could I.

"Perfect," I manage to choke out rather happily.

She nods her head, still smiling. "I'm done at 5 today, so, I'll meet you down here, and we can walk into town."

"Great, see you at 5," I confirm, swiftly turning on my heels and fleeing out the door. I laugh at what she must think of me, practically running away from the woman I just asked out, but then again, that's all I've been doing lately - running away.

No matter how far I run, I can't seem to get far enough away from the demons chasing me. I want to be free of them. I really do, but I'm not sure how.

A constant cloud of confusion and agony hang over me. I shouldn't have asked her out. I shouldn't have allowed myself the chance to do something for me. Yet, no amount of guilt could keep me from blurting out the words.

It's just drinks, I remind myself. Drinks don't mean anything, and they definitely don't mean I have to enjoy myself.

A Famous Kind of Love

Five

London

I must be dreaming. I have to be dreaming. There's no other way to explain what just happened. Jameson Decker, movie star, just asked me out.

At least, I think that's what just happened. I mean his expression after the words came out of his mouth was slightly confusing. He looked like he might vomit or maybe like he wanted to take it all back.

Heck, maybe he did? But who the hell cares?

Certainly not me. No, I'm far too excited by the fact that he even felt the need to ask me out for drinks. Maybe it was out of pity? Or maybe it was out of desperation to have some personal contact after locking himself away in his room for four days? Who knows?

What I do know is it's something a girl like me could only dream about, and I'm sure as hell not going to say no to my personal Cinderella story, even if there will be no happy ending for me.

I suppose there could be a happy ending, but I'm not stupid enough to allow myself to think that way. At least, not again.

I won't allow myself to be taken advantage of, to think that this beautiful, wealthy man could actually want a woman like me. I thought that about Brayden's dad, Hamish, and look where I ended up - a single mom living paycheck to paycheck.

It's not like I'm not used to it. It's how I grew up. My dad left when I was barely old enough to remember him, and my mom was stuck with me. She moved back in with her parents and worked her ass off to make ends meet.

I always swore my life would be different. I was going to marry a man who loved me, and my children would never have to worry about anything.

I know that's why I fell for the first man I met that whispered sweet promises into my ear. I learned the hard way that promises like that don't mean shit, and that poor women like me are destined to repeat their parents' lives.

It's okay though. I know who I am and what my life entails. I accepted that this is what the rest of my life will look like, and honestly, I'm good with it. I don't need fancy or extravagant. I just need this small town, my friends, and my son.

I force myself to move away from the counter and back into my office where my phone lays on my desk, waiting for me to text Sabrina and ask her to take care of Brayden tonight so I can live out my own fantasy.

Once I'm in my office and have successfully typed out my text, I get back to the never-ending pile of paperwork on my desk, hoping the next several hours go by fast and knowing there's no way in hell I will get that lucky.

My life has been filled with bad luck. My grandparents never really wanted anything to do with me and died before I was ten. My mom died before Brayden was born, and I have no clue who my father is. I got pregnant from the first guy I slept with, then he ran so fast I'm pretty sure I got whiplash. Oh, and let's not forget all the guys that have graced my life since.

I know my life could have been far worse, but it still wasn't great. None of that stops me from being as positive as possible though.

That's one thing I always promised myself I would do - be positive. My mom was always a Negative Nancy, never happy with anything in life and certainly never appreciative of what she had. It had made me furious that she would want to live her life that way.

She was always complaining about work or having to take care of me. Not that she ever really took care of me. Even after my grandparents died, she left me pretty much on my own. And, when she did spend time with me, it always involved pointing out all the ways I was like my father and how much that bothered her.

In fact, I don't think I ever really saw my mom smile.

I know her life wasn't the best, but still, mine isn't either. That doesn't mean I shouldn't be grateful for what I do have.

My phone vibrates on the metal top of my desk, letting me know that Sabrina has replied. I pick it up to read her text and laugh.

Sabrina: Sure, I can do that. But I'm curious as to why you need me to watch him tonight. Got a hot date planned? ;)

Me: Something like that.

Sabrina: I want all the details now.

Me: Can't right now. Working.

Sabrina: Well, I better get them today at some point.

Me: You know I don't kiss and tell.

Sabrina: Wait, have you kissed someone?

Me: No, but you know what I meant.

Sabrina: Yea, yea, whatever. See you when you pick up B.

I place my phone back down on the desk and get back to work. The busier I am, the faster the time will go by.

And true enough, before I know it, five o'clock has rolled around and my body is racing with the kind of giddy excitement I haven't felt since I was a child on Christmas morning.

I wrap up what I'm working on in my office and head out to the lobby, my multitude of bags hanging on my arm. I don't know what I expect to see when I round the corner, but Jamie leaning against the counter looking sexy as hell is not one of them.

I make my way to where he stands. He doesn't move as my bags smack together with the sway of my hips. His face is set in a pout, appearing deep in thought, and making me wonder what is going on in that head of his. I inch closer and closer, my numerous bags still making an endless amount of noise, yet he still stands like a brooding statue.

There's no hint of emotion on his face unless you count the sour look on his lips, as if he's thinking about something that upsets him. I desperately hope it's not our evening together that he's thinking about. Damn would that be a hit to my ego.

"Is the prospect of having drinks with me really that terrible?" I joke, hoping to finally get his attention.

He looks up, his mouth relaxing into a subtle smile. "Sorry, I didn't hear you."

"I can see that," I note, tilting my head in his direction. "Shall we?"

"Yea." He pushes himself off the counter as we make our way across the lobby. "Do you mind if we just grab drinks in the hotel bar tonight? I'm not really in the mood to venture into town," he admits rather stoically.

"Sure," I say, leading the way towards the bar behind the restaurant. We wander through the lobby, down the hallway, and off to the right that leads to the restaurant and bar. "I guess I could have left these in my office." I laugh, holding my arm up to show Jamie the bags.

"Oh, I didn't even notice them on your arm. Do you want me to carry them?"

I look over my shoulder at him. "It's quite chivalrous of you to offer, but it's not necessary."

We turn the corner into the bar, and I holler one of the waiters over, asking him to place my stuff behind the bar. Then, I motion for Jamie to sit down with me.

He's barely said a word the entire time. Well, other than asking if he can carry my bags, which was both shocking and sweet at the same time. Of all the people in the world I thought would offer to carry my bags, a movie star was not one of them.

He takes a seat effortlessly on the bar stool while I do an awkward hop to get my butt up on the stool.

He chuckles, looking slyly over his shoulder at me.

"What? I'm short. It's hard for me to get on these things," I say, spinning on the stool so I'm facing him and the bar now.

"You're cute," he states. It's not flirty, but there's some amusement behind his words that sends heat to my cheeks.

"I assume that's a good thing."

He nods his head slowly. "It's definitely not a bad thing."

I give him a shy smile, studying his dark eyes. They look like my favorite things - chocolate and rum mixed together, creating a smooth golden-brown color. Hints of excitement and passion hide behind the clouds of sorrow in his eyes. I stare deep into them, feeling a hurricane of emotions whip through me. They tell me everything I want to know about him while also hiding it all at the same time.

I can't look away no matter how hard I want to, and memories of the spark I felt when our hands touched flash across my mind. How can a man I barely know make me feel so keyed up and comfortable at the same time? That spark between us makes me feel alive, feel things I never thought I'd feel.

The thump of a hand on the oak bar counter pulls me from my thoughts and forces my eyes from his. "Hey boss, what can I get ya this evening?"

"Ray, good to see you, but you know I'm not your boss," I correct him, warmth in my words.

"Maybe not directly, but you're my boss' boss, so same thing." He shrugs his shoulders, while he pours me a glass of rum and coke - my favorite.

He sets the glass in front of me. "Thank you," I say, lifting the glass to him.

"And for you?" he asks Jamie.

"I'll have what she's having." He points his head to me.

Ray's eyes dart between the two of us, and I can see the curiosity in them, but he doesn't say anything. Instead, he pours another drink, hands it to Jamie, and walks away.

Jamie tips the glass to his lips and swallows. "I wouldn't have pegged you for a rum and coke kind of gal."

"That's the thing about me. I'm full of surprises." Our eyes meet, and I know in that instant that he feels it too - whatever this electricity or fire is between us.

I won't lie, I'm terrified of this feeling. The man in front of me is a complete stranger, and yet, he has me all twisted up inside. I want nothing more than to get to know him better in every way that counts, which is exactly what I plan to do for the next couple hours.

"So," I say not sure where to start, my nerves kicking up a notch and making me sweat.

He glances my way, his eyes gazing deep into my soul. "So," he mimics.

"Is it just me or is this a little weird?" I chuckle awkwardly, a small squeak coming through.

He follows suit. "It's definitely a little weird, but it's a good kind of weird." He takes a small sip of his drink while I down the rest of mine.

"Hit me with another one, Ray!" I demand, slamming the glass on the counter. I need all the liquid courage I can get if I'm going to make it through this night.

Ray sets a new drink in front of me, and I turn on my bar stool to face Jamie. "Let's play a game."

"Okay." He nods, leaning his arm on the bar and propping his head in his hand.

"It's called My Favorite Things. You have 30 seconds to list off your favorite things for each category," I explain.

He squeezes his brows together, creating defined wrinkles on his forehead. *Gosh, even his wrinkles are hot.* "I've never heard of this game," he says.

I point my finger at him and smirk. "That's because I just made it up."

He laughs, deep and hearty. "Got it. What are the categories?"

"Food, Movies, Music, Things to Do, and Places to Travel," I count them off on one hand.

"Let's do it," he agrees, laying his phone out on the bar and pulling up the timer. He turns to me, his unusually white teeth making his smile seem brighter. "You're up first."

"Food," I state, and he sets the timer. "Burgers, fries, pizza…pasta, salad," I pause trying to think of more.

"Time," he says. "My turn. Sushi, pizza, burgers, steak, lobster, shrimp, caviar."

"Eh," I cut him off, mimicking a timer. "Now, movies. Ready?" He nods his head and taps the timer once again. "Sweet Home Alabama, A Cinderella Story, Forever My Girl, Where the Heart Is, Pretty…"

"Beep!" He lets out dramatically.

"I wasn't done yet," I whine, having about twenty more movies on my favorites list.

"You're the one who made up the rules." He shrugs his shoulders and states, "Action movies."

I tip my head towards his phone. "But you didn't start the

timer."

"I didn't need to."

"You can't just say action movies," I insist, sipping on my drink.

"But I love all action movies," he counters, making me want to smack the snark out of him.

I roll my eyes. "Fine, what's the best action movie you've ever watched?"

"By the Dim Light of Night," he states.

"Isn't that one of the first action movies you made? I believe you were working with a girl's father to save the girl from some gang?"

"Yea, I loved making that movie. It was before I started getting gigs with larger production companies. The whole team was down-to-earth and cool to work with."

I tap my finger on my chin. "Interesting."

"Yea, anyway, let's get back to the game." He grins and taps his phone, bringing it back to life.

We continue playing the game for the next few minutes, learning a little bit more about each other. I find out he enjoys classic rock, basketball, football, and traveling the world. I also learn that for as many things that are different about us, we have just as many things in common, something I wouldn't expect to have with a celebrity.

Six

Jamie

I don't know why I'm wandering through the lobby looking for her, but this is the fifth time I've come down here today, trying to catch a glimpse of the woman currently haunting my dreams and hoping to run into her like I did the other day.

Ah, the other day, when I asked her out for drinks. I had no idea what I was getting myself into, but it was worth it. I haven't enjoyed myself like that in what feels like an eternity.

And London was so much more than any woman I ever spent time with before. She's not just sexy as hell, but she's also witty, fun, kind, and exceptionally creative. That game she came up with turned out to be entertaining and made all the small talk a lot less like a chore.

I left that bar feeling somewhat hopeful and excited to see her again.

It doesn't matter that I have nothing to give her. My body and my mind are on separate wavelengths. No matter how many times I remind myself I'm too broken and not worthy of happiness, I still have the urge to see her, to touch her, and to feel those plush pink lips on mine.

I glance at the front desk, waiting to see that long blond hair and those gorgeous ocean blue eyes and hoping to hear that musical laugh of hers. But once again, she's not there. In fact, no one's there at all.

I scan the lobby, making sure no one else is in here or recognizes me. When my eyes hit the front desk again, I notice the young girl from my first day here. She looks just as freaked out now as she did then.

I know it's the disguise I wear. I do it on purpose to keep people from coming too close to recognizing me, and it works for the most part.

I venture over to the desk. "Is London in today?" I catch myself asking before I can stop myself.

The girl shakes her head. "Today's her day off. Is there something I can help you with?" she asks.

"No, thanks, I'm good," I answer, walking away from the

counter.

My hand absentmindedly reaches into my front pocket, pulling out the business card she gave me. I rub my fingers over London's phone number. I can't even begin to count how many times I've done this over the last few days. I want to save it in my phone and use it, but I know it's such a bad idea.

I continue to walk through the lobby, finding myself heading towards the door rather than back up to my room. I push it open, letting the sunshine hit my face for the first time in days. I feel like a bear coming out of hibernation by the way my eyes squint through my sunglasses.

My legs carry me up the sidewalk towards Main Street. Google Maps tells me it's about 1.5 miles to the center of town, but that's okay. I need the fresh air and exercise.

The closer I get to town, the more people I see out on the road and sidewalk. I'm not used to the friendly smiles or the happy "hellos" that come my way. No one stops to ask for a picture or an autograph. Instead, they all act like I'm just another person in town. Hell, maybe I am to them.

I don't know what to do with that or how to feel about it. It's the complete opposite from LA streets. I'd never dream of walking down the streets of LA unprotected. I don't think I ever have, actually. Too many people come out hoping to see someone famous, and way too many of them take it over the top.

Historic buildings line Main Street. I can tell they've been updated over the years, but their natural French architecture remains. Store fronts peek out from underneath awnings and patio coverings.

I'm surprised by how many stores occupy these buildings, and they're not generic ones either. They each have their own unique specialties.

Up ahead, a bright yellow and pale blue sign catches my eye: The Sunrise Cafe. The quaint, little coffee shop seems to be busting at the seams with people. Both inside and out, people stand around with coffee and pastries in-hand.

It's probably the one place I shouldn't go into because I have a higher chance of being recognized, but the smell of coffee on the breeze is too amazing to pass up. I suck in a deep breath, feeling a grumble in my stomach, and quickly cross the street to the cafe before I can change my mind.

I pull my baseball cap a little lower before stepping inside. Surprisingly, the line isn't long, and I have my coffee and croissant rather quickly.

I step away from the counter, searching the cafe when my eyes land on a familiar head of blond hair, and I will her to look in my direction. I can't stop the smile that instantly crosses my face when I see her. I wish I knew what it was about her that affects me this way.

Her eyes land on me, and her face lights up with a bright smile. She waves me over, and I make my way through the crowded cafe. It isn't until I'm standing next to the table that I realize there's a boy sitting with her. He can't be more than eight years old, and his dark hair contrasts with his mother's lighter hair.

"Hey," she says. "Didn't expect to see you here."

"I didn't expect to be here, but I needed to get out of the hotel," I respond, shifting on my feet lightly. I'm not sure whether to sit down or not. Even though she waved me over, I don't want to simply assume she was inviting me to join them.

London must notice my inner turmoil because she waves towards the empty chair. "Please, join us."

I feel awkward taking the seat across from her putting me next to the boy I assume is her son. "It's okay. I don't want to intrude."

London shakes her head. "You won't be intruding. We'd love to have someone else to talk to, wouldn't we, B?"

The boy nods his head eagerly. "Yea, it gets boring just the two of us all the time."

"Gee, thanks, kid," London scoffs, crossing her arms in front of her.

He giggles and nibbles on his breakfast sandwich, shrugging his shoulders.

London turns back to me. "See, we'd love for you to join. So, take a seat." She points to the chair next to the boy again.

I laugh at her insistent tone but do as she says. I'm more of the take charge kind of guy, but I have no qualms with letting a woman tell me what to do. I can thank my grandma for that.

I sit in the chair and sip on my coffee, not sure what to say. I bounce my legs up and down, feeling completely out of place here.

"This is my son, Brayden." London points to the boy next to me. "Brayden, this is Jamie."

Brayden turns to me with his hand stretched out for me to shake. "Nice to meet you, Jamie," he says, his eyes growing wide when he realizes who I am. "Wait, you're that Jamie. I've seen all your movies. You're like my favorite actor ever." He tries to keep his voice even and calm, but I don't miss the enthusiasm pouring off his face.

I smile, shaking his hand. I should be concerned about the fact he knows who I am, but oddly, I'm not. "Well, thanks. It's nice to meet you too, Brayden."

"Mama says you're staying at the hotel. Are you on vacation? Or are you done making movies forever? If that's true, I'd be so sad." He frowns.

My mind doesn't even process what he's saying, instead, it focuses on the fact that London has been talking about me. At least, I'm not the only one feeling whatever this is.

I look at her, smirking. "Oh really, she's been talking about me?"

Her face darkens about twenty shades of red, and she gives me a sheepish smile. "I've been discrete thank you very much. And to be fair, I only told him you were a guest at our hotel. He's the one who made the connection."

"Ah," I say, nodding my head and lifting my eyebrows.

"It's true," Brayden confirms. "She asked if I was okay with you sitting with us. I'm definitely okay with you sitting with us now that I know who you are!"

"Well, I'm glad you decided I could join." I smile at him.

He chews on a bite of sandwich and swallows quickly. "Mama says we should always invite people to be our friends, especially if they don't have many."

I laugh, slightly offended, even though it's true. I don't have many friends, not genuine ones anyway.

"Brayden," London whispers loudly, trying to kick him under the table.

She misses though and kicks me in the shin, a sharp pain shooting up my leg.

"Geesh woman, what did I do?" I joke, pretending to be hurt.

Her eyes widen, and she freezes. "Oh my goodness, did I just kick you?"

I nod, trying to hide my laughter.

Her hands cup her cheeks. "I am so sorry. I totally meant that for Brayden." I don't think her cheeks could get any redder at this point.

"Hey, what did I do?" Brayden pipes up.

London glances over at him. "You told the man he has no friends," she explains, flabbergasted.

"Yea, so?" he questions, his brows crinkled together, clearly confused.

"It's not nice to say things like that, B. Remember how we

always talk about the power of words? We have to be careful with how we use them."

He nods, a frown on his face. His eyes peer up at me. "I'm sorry if I hurt your feelings, Mr. Jamie."

I put my hand on his shoulder. "Don't worry about it. You didn't hurt my feelings, but your mom is right. You definitely should watch how you use your words."

"Yes sir," he mutters, munching on a hash brown from his plate.

London mouths the words "thank you" to me and smiles.

A sudden wave of guilt hits me. I shouldn't feel this happy, not when I took another family's happiness from them. The sudden urge to rush out hits, and I quickly excuse myself and get as far away from happiness as possible.

Even if it was an accident, it's what I deserve. I deserve to know what this family will feel like for the rest of their lives.

Lonely. Sad. Empty. Broken.

Seven

London

Jamie's sudden need to rush out of the cafe leaves me feeling empty and completely confused. Did I do or say something wrong?

I didn't miss the way his face paled or the panic in his eyes. I mean all I did was say thank you for his help in reinforcing my message to B, but maybe I shouldn't have?

I shake my head. This is nonsense. What does it matter why he ran out of here? It doesn't, not when I have a rare whole day off to spend with my son.

We walk down main street, enjoying the warm sun on our backs. Brayden's school year will be starting soon, and these days will become fewer and farther between. Thankfully, I still have a couple weeks left to make the most of this summer. Although, I have no doubts work will get in the way of the time we do have, and Brayden will have to spend time with Ki or Sabrina when he's not at summer camp.

I hate that I have to do that, but I need this job to make sure Brayden has everything he needs. Unfortunately, to do that, I have to go running when the boss calls. I'm just grateful that Brayden has surrogate aunts that love to spend time with him when I'm working.

"So, B, what shall we do for the rest of the day?" I ask, putting my arm around his shoulders. I still can't believe that at eight years old he's almost as tall as me.

He puts his finger on his chin and tilts his head toward me. "Hm, I'm not sure. What about the beach?" he asks.

I squeeze his shoulders. "I think that's a great idea. Do we need bathing suits today or are we just walking?"

"Well, bathing suits would mean we have to go home and change, but walking means we'll collect shells, and we don't have any bags."

"I'm sure we can find a bag somewhere, but you're right. We'd have to change before we could get in the water," I agree, wondering when my son became old enough to be so logical. He's so much wiser than his eight years old, and I wonder if that has to do with the fact it's always been just the two of us.

"Let's just walk. We can always walk through the waves to

cool off," he finally decides, clearly having put great thought into it.

"Sounds perfect," I respond, guiding him towards the beach. It's not too far from Main Street, just a couple blocks over.

That's the beauty of Sunrise, almost everything is within walking distance, which comes in handy when you have a shitty old rust bucket like I do for a car. And on days like this with the bright sun beating down and a cool ocean breeze, walking is the best option.

We continue our trek down to the beach. Brayden talks my ear off about school starting and all the fun things he's been doing at summer camp. It's refreshing to hear my usually shy and quiet son so animated and excited about all the friends he's made.

"Johnny even told me I could come over to his house this weekend for a camp out. His dad makes hot dogs and s'mores, and they play games and tell stories over a little campfire. It sounds like lots of fun. Ya think I can go?" he asks, quirking his head up at me as we step out onto the beach.

We both bend down to slip off our shoes. "We might be able to do that, but I'd like to talk to his parents first," I say, standing back up slightly out of breath.

"Okay," he answers enthusiastically. The smile across his face makes me feel so happy and alive inside.

I ruffle his hair and can't help the answering smile that forms on my face. I always worry that I'm not enough, that I can't give him everything he needs in life but seeing him so enthusiastic helps tamper that worry down some.

I can't change the fact his father left before he was born, and honestly, I'm not sure I'd want to. His father was just a rich jackass with no respect for anyone but himself. However, I do wish Brayden had someone in his life that he could look up to, someone to show him how a man behaves.

I know he has Hunter and his friends' dads, but it's not the same and I know that. I'm so grateful for the men he does have in his life, especially Hunter. He loves to take Brayden out fishing, and I know it means the world to him. I just wish things had turned out different with the men in my life.

We start our walk out onto the beach, my feet sinking in the sand with each step I take. I love the feel of the tiny, rough particles between my toes.

We make our way down to the waterline and begin our walk up the shore. The water is a little rough today thanks to the wind, but not nearly enough to bring the surfers out.

"Mom, look! It's a jellyfish." Brayden points to the slimy, white tentacled creature in the sand just ahead of us.

Jellyfish are only one of the many reasons I'm not too fond of venturing into the water. Honestly, I'm surprised I do make it out into the waves with the amount of dead jellyfish I've found on the beach over the years. It's just so hard to tell my son no sometimes.

"And there's a horseshoe crab shell over there." He points up on the shore where a pile of driftwood and seaweed sit. "Can we take it home?" he asks.

"No, do you know how gross those things are? Not to mention, they stink." I scrunch my nose up at the thought. I remember when my mom thought it'd be cool to take one of those home with us. It was one of the few days she actually spent with me growing up.

She decided to take me to the beach. As we were walking, we saw one of the horseshoe crabs on the sand. She picked it up and claimed we were going to take it home with us. Except, she accidentally left it in the scorching hot car. The worst part was the smell that didn't go away for days.

I smile at one of the few good memories I have of my mom. I didn't know back then that I'd cherish that moment as much as I do now.

"Ugh, you're no fun," Brayden whines and I laugh.

"I'm plenty fun," I state, picking up a pile of wet sand and tossing it at him.

"Mom," he screams, glaring at me. A big splat of brown sand sits in the center of his chest. I cover my mouth, hiding my laughter.

He brushes off the sand, mumbling something about how that wasn't cool. Then, he reaches down and grabs a handful of sand. I know exactly what he's about to do. "Don't you dare, B. I'll ground you," I squeal, running in the opposite direction.

"No, you won't," he hollers over the roar of the waves just before I feel a big *splat* on my back.

I turn around, laughing and picking up more sand as Brayden does the same. We squeal, laugh, and toss sand at each other for what feels like forever before I yell, "Let's call a truce. I need to take a breather."

"Deal," he agrees, plopping down in the dry sand just behind us. "I'm tired."

"Me too, kid," I say, joining him.

"But it was pretty fun." He smiles up at me.

"Yea, it was."

We sit there in silence, staring out at the waves for a few minutes. Brayden chews on the corner of his mouth, and I know he's thinking about something serious. I hate that he worries so much, and it makes me feel like a terrible mom that my son is so much more grown up than he should be.

Ki and Sabrina assure me that's not a bad thing, that some children are just born that way, but it doesn't make me feel any better.

"Mom," he finally says, his questioning eyes staring a hole into my skin.

"Yea, buddy?"

"I just... thank you."

I look at him, my brows furrowed together. I wish I knew what was going through his head right now. "For what?" I ask.

"For being my mom and my dad. I know it's hard for you to do everything."

I don't know where this is coming from, but tears pool around my eyes. I wrap my arm around his shoulder and pull him in close. "It's not as hard as you might think. You're my world, B, that makes it easy to do everything I can for you. I love everything about being your mom but thank you for saying that."

He leans his head on my shoulder. "I know, but my camp counselor said we should always thank the people who work the hardest for us. I haven't said thank you in a while, so I thought I should."

"I love you, B."

"Love you too, Mom."

It's rare for Brayden to want to be held or even be this close to me anymore, so I soak in this whole moment for as long as I can. I hate that his father was such a pretentious jackass and didn't want anything to do with me or him, but as I hug my son closer to me, I know that he's the one missing out on us.

Eight

Jamie

This is my problem. Every time I start to feel anything close to happiness, the past comes rushing back to me, reminding me of everything I took from that family.

How can I possibly live *my* life knowing that I took one?

I know it was an accident. Shit, everyone keeps reminding me of that, but it doesn't change the very real facts.

I hurt an eight-year-old girl - a girl who'd barely begun to live. How does anyone come back from that?

They don't, not when they're haunted by the ghosts and all of the what ifs.

What if I'd been paying more attention? What if I'd swerved the other way?

Logically, I know I did everything I could, but logic doesn't have a place in my thoughts - not now, not ever.

I lean my head against the wing-backed chair in my room, rubbing my temples. The curtains are closed, and the lights are shut off. The only bit of light entering the room shines through the cracks around the curtains.

I stare into the dark nothing of the curtains, replaying the accident over and over and letting it consume me.

I don't know how long I've been hiding in the dark or when I ate last. It's been at least 24 hours, that much I do know, but other than that, I don't really give two fucks.

I shouldn't be alive anyway. I should have been the one to die in that accident, and that precious little girl should have lived.

But maybe the big man upstairs had a bigger plan, one I can't quite see. It's not like I set out that night to hurt anyone. The sad fact is I didn't. I simply lost control of my car.

My phone rings for the thousandth time on the table beside me, but I ignore it. I'm not in the mood to talk to whoever the hell it is. I'd much rather sit in the dark with my sins.

A soft knock on the door jolts me out of my depressive state. I stand, knowing Damon called the hotel to check on me. I may have been ignoring his calls, but I did check to see who was calling in the first place.

I open the door, not even bothering to check the peephole first. Probably a stupid mistake on my part, but it won't be the worst one I've made.

Swinging the door wide, my eyes land on the angelic face of London. Her features are soft with empathy, and her brows are wrinkled with concern. "I got a call from your manager. He asked me to check on you," she whispers, twisting her hands together.

I motion for her to come in. She shakes her head, stepping into the room and flipping on the lights. I'm sure I look like a mess.

"How long have you been in those clothes?" she asks, wrinkling her nose up in disgust.

I look down to see brown stains splattered on the front of my shirt, and I honestly can't remember what they're from.

She tilts her head to the side. "Jamie, what's going on? Clearly, you're not okay."

"I'm fine," I mumble, pushing past her and back to the chair.

"So, you make a habit of living in the dark, not taking a shower, and not eating for days?" she asks, sitting down on the couch in the living area, probably trying to get as far away from my stench as possible.

"It hasn't been days," I mutter, staring at a small speck of fuzz on the floor. I don't know why it stands out to me, but anything is better than looking at the woman judging me right now.

"Yes, it has," she says, standing and crossing her arms in front of her. "We're going to talk more about this, but first, you're going to take a shower and change your damn clothes. Because I can't sit any longer in this room with you smelling like garbage."

I glare at her, challenging her words, but her eyes are much harder, chastising me for living this way. I give in, standing from the chair and heading towards the bathroom. I stop at my suitcase on the way, grabbing some clean clothes. Then, I huff my way reluctantly into the bathroom.

A mere ten minutes later, I'm standing in front of London again, towel drying my hair and wearing clean clothes.

"Much better," she says from her place on the couch. She pats the space next to her and I take a seat. "Now, care to explain, why you've holed yourself up in your bedroom?"

"It doesn't matter. Nothing matters anymore," I mutter.

She studies my face, and I study her eyes. She's trying to read me, but I know she can't. Her bright blue eyes search mine for any hint of clarification. She wants to say something, I can see that, but she doesn't. Instead, her face twists with a million different emotions.

We sit there in silence for a while before she stands. "It's not any of my business. Just do me a favor and call your manager to let him know you're okay," she says, slightly angry.

She starts towards the door. Something inside me wants to stop her. I want nothing more than to be left alone, and yet I want her here as well.

"Please don't go," I blurt out just as her hand reaches the door handle.

She stops, turning slowly on her heels. "I'm not going to stay simply to watch you wallow in whatever this is," she says, shaking her head and looking at me with a face full of pity.

That pity is the reason I want to be left alone. I hate having people look at me like they feel sorry for me, like they want to cry when they see me sitting alone in the dark. But I also don't want to be alone. I don't want to be left alone with my feelings, afraid of where this dark hole might take me.

At least if she's here, I can forget about it all, even if only for a few minutes.

"I know I'm a mess, but I'd rather not be alone right now. Can you just come sit with me for a bit?"

She sighs, "Jamie, I have to get back to work. I shouldn't even be up here right now checking on you. I wouldn't do this for anyone else."

My ears perk up with a twinge of hope, but I squash it down quickly. "If you wouldn't normally do this for others, why do it for me?" I ask, needing to quench my curiosity.

She strides over to me, settling down on the couch next to me. "I wish I knew the answer to that. There's just something about you that keeps bringing me back."

"I feel the same way," I admit before I have time to think about what I'm saying. Those words shouldn't have come out of my mouth no matter how true they are to me.

London grabs my hands in hers and rubs her fingers across the back of them. "I know we barely know each other, but I want to help you. I can see something is going on inside that head of yours."

"Yea, but you can't help with that. I'm not sure anyone can," I grumble the last part.

She moves in closer to me, her body almost flush against mine. I know she's just trying to comfort me, but my dick hardens instantly. "What about a counselor?" And there it goes, that damn word again - counselor.

I want to argue, fight her on this subject, but her eyes, full of innocence, sear my skin and make me bounce the word around inside my head. Is it a coincidence that both my manager and a stranger think I need to see a counselor? As much as I hate to admit it, maybe there is something to both their suggestions.

"I'm not big on counselors," I finally speak.

Her fingertips brush against my arm. "I don't think anyone really is, but sometimes, it's something you need to do, whether you want to or not."

I nod my head slowly, letting her words seep into my mind. "Know any good counselors?" I laugh nervously, scratching the back of my neck.

"Yea, there's a good one right in town." She smiles, reaching for the pen and pad on the coffee table and writing a number down. She leans back, the heat from her skin penetrating the icy walls around my heart.

I want so bad to lean in and taste her lips on mine, but I

shouldn't. This feels like such an intimate moment, one I'm not sure I want to ruin.

Shit, I don't even know if she knows about the accident, and I don't want to bring it up. Although, I'm sure she saw all the tabloid stories. They were plastered everywhere, but then again, maybe she doesn't read them?

If she does though, she wouldn't want me to kiss her anyway.

Her hands find my cheeks, cupping them in the softest hug possible. She must notice the agony twisting my face into a thousand tiny wrinkles. She leans in, bringing her face to meet mine. "Whatever you need, Jamie, I'm here."

Those words wash away all sanity as I lean my head closer to hers. Our lips meet softly at first, brushing lightly against each other, slowly turning into something more fierce, needy.

My arms wrap around her waist, pulling her in tighter to me. My lips move over hers as if they've done it a thousand times. She tastes like caramel, chocolate, and everything sweet and good in this world. I can't get enough of her.

I pull her in even closer, shifting her onto my lap. The entire time our lips stay connected, and our tongues mingle like old friends. My hands roam up and down her waist, learning every curve.

She pulls back, breathing hard. "Wow, that was…" she pauses, searching for the words.

I know what she means. That kiss was fucking incredible and a huge mistake. My face hardens and my body goes rigid as I put up my armor. "A mistake. I shouldn't have done that," I say, moving out from underneath her.

Her eyes widen with shock, and I see tears glistening around the rim. I know I upset her, but I had to. No matter how amazing that kiss was, it can never happen again.

She slides off my lap, her eyes downcast. "I think I should go," she whispers just before fleeing from my room.

Nine

London

I pull the door shut behind me, letting only a few tears fall. That was the most explosive make-out session I've ever had, and I know he felt it too. Shoot, I felt his hard-on under my leg.

But then he says it was a mistake, that it should have never happened. And maybe it shouldn't have happened in that exact moment, but nothing about that kiss was a mistake, absolutely nothing.

I shift my blouse, releasing the wrinkles in it and force myself to walk towards the elevator. Even if I just had the most incredible kiss of my life, I still have a job to do.

Once I'm back in the lobby, I head to my office, spending the rest of the day with my face buried in paperwork. Too bad it doesn't help me forget anything about his kiss.

Before I know it, my phone buzzes with the reminder to pick B up from summer camp. With how busy my days are, I have to set a reminder to make sure I don't get so caught up in work that I'm late.

I look at the clock, hardly believing it's almost five already. I gather up my stuff and rush out of the hotel.

I don't dare go check on Jamie before I leave. That's all I'd need - a reminder of his dark expression telling me it should have never happened. No thanks.

Instead, I climb into my car and focus my attention on getting Brayden. The summer camp isn't far from the hotel, just a few miles outside town. I'd always heard good things about the camp, but I had been so nervous about sending him. I'm glad I took the chance though because he's enjoying himself for once.

I pull up into the pickup area and see Brayden talking animatedly with his friends. I smile, so grateful that my typically weary and nervous boy is having fun. One of the camp counselors lets him know I'm here, and he rushes to the car, swinging the door open and sliding into the back seat.

"Hey buddy," I say, peering at him over the seat.

"Hey, mom, did you see me over there talking to my friends?"

"Yea, I did," I nod, pulling out of the parking lot and back onto the main road.

"They're so cool, and they invited me over for dinner tomorrow night. The one standing next to me with the curly hair was Johnny. He's the one that invited me for a sleepover sometime." He's talking so fast I can barely make out what he's saying. "So, can I go?" he asks abruptly.

I've barely had time to process what he just said. "Go where?" I question, glancing at him in the rear-view mirror.

He huffs, slumping down in his seat, the seatbelt sliding up to his throat. "To dinner with my friends tomorrow."

I look back to the road. "B, sit up so your seatbelt isn't strangling you, please. And yes, if you let me know the details, I'm sure we can make it happen."

He squeals loudly. "Yes! Thank you, thank you, thank you. Mom, you're the best."

I laugh softly, making a sharp right turn into the little cul de sac we live in. I park the car in the driveway of our modest, one-story, three-bedroom house. There really isn't anything special about it except that it's the same house I grew up in, left to me when my mom passed away. In fact, it looks like most of the other houses in our little neighborhood - bland shutters, gray siding, and a simple black door, but even in its simplicity, it's perfect to me.

Brayden hops out of the car, racing to the door. I shake my head. I don't know why he's in such a hurry. It's not like he has a house key on him.

Once we're inside, I head straight to the kitchen, looking

through the cabinets for dinner. "Brayden," I yell. "What do you want to eat tonight?"

He doesn't respond. Instead, I hear his feet pitter pattering across the hardwood floor just before his head peeks into the kitchen. "Pizza!" he exclaims.

"We don't have pizza." I frown.

"Can we order out?" his eyes are hopeful, but he knows the rules.

"B, we only order out on Saturdays, remember? I can't afford to do it more than that."

I hate that my son is aware of our money struggles, but he's a boy who needs to know every reason why. Sometimes, explaining it to him is better than keeping it from him.

He looks at me, his mouth twisted up in thought. "Well, I really want pizza," he whines. "Wait, I know we can order pizza tonight and not order food on Saturday," he says, excitedly.

"What about dinner tomorrow night with your friends?" I ask, not sure if they'll be eating out or not.

"That's at Carter's house. His mom is making dinner," he explains.

I take a deep breath. "Okay, then, I suppose we can have pizza for dinner tonight."

Brayden jumps up and down and yells, "This is the best day ever!" He runs out of the kitchen before I can even ask what kind of pizza he wants.

Pepperoni it is.

I smile, grateful that my son gets excited over the smallest things and also sad that I've had to raise him that way. I grew up the same way with nothing to our name except this house and an old car that barely ran when we needed it to.

I always swore my child wouldn't grow up that way, but life clearly had other plans.

The day I found out I was pregnant was the same day I realized I was never going to get to do all the things I'd dreamed of - college, run my own business, or make something of myself.

At nineteen, there was absolutely no way I'd be able to provide my child with everything I never had, not when I was barely out of high school and a maid making minimum wage at the same damn hotel I'm still working at now.

It's okay though. We're okay, and Brayden has everything he needs. That's the important thing. We may not get to do a lot of super cool things or go on nice vacations every year, but we don't lack the essentials we need to live.

However, I do wish that he didn't have to know these realities at such a young age. The older he gets, though, the harder it is to hide the fact that money isn't easy to come by. I just keep reminding myself that all of this will come in handy for him one day. At least, I hope so.

I reach for my phone and dial the closest pizza shop that delivers to Sunrise. When our order is placed, I lay my phone down on the counter and go about emptying the dishwasher and cleaning up the kitchen.

My phone buzzes, making me jump. I pick it up, thinking it's the pizza guy needing better directions, which happens a lot more than one would expect.

But the message from the unknown number isn't the pizza guy.

I know because I didn't have an intense make out session on the pizza guy's lap and he didn't tell me it was a mistake, so there'd be no reason for the text to apologize "about earlier today".

My heart pounds harder and faster, and my breathing grows heavy. I click on the message.

Unknown: I'm sorry about earlier today. I shouldn't have done that, but I also shouldn't have treated you the way I did either. You deserve better than me.

That's it?

I deserve better?

My thoughts fly through my mind, my emotions on as wild of a ride as my thoughts. I can't contain them as I try to make sense of it all. Anger pulses through my veins and my fingers tighten their grip on my phone.

What does he mean by I deserve better? He doesn't know shit about me, so how could he possibly know what I deserve? And why the hell does every guy I date think they get to decide what's best for me? Well, except Hamish, he left us because it was best for him, but still, I think I've earned the damn right to decide what I deserve.

Ten

Jamie

I stare at the bright phone screen, London's name shining in my face. Three dots appear and then disappear several times, but she never responds.

Did I really expect her to?

No, I didn't, but if I'm being honest, a little part of me hoped she would. I don't know what that part of me expected her to say though. I didn't really give her much room to protest.

Although, I guess I thought maybe she'd at least say it's okay.

Even though I know it's not okay. Nothing about this entire

situation is okay, unfortunately. And, I don't have a fucking clue how to change that.

My eyes land on the notepad in front of me. The black writing stands out in protest against the sheer white paper. I do know how to change this. I need to get some damn help.

I pick up my phone, typing the numbers in quickly before I have a chance to rethink this. A soft female voice answers right after the first ring. "Sunrise Counseling Services, this is Tina. How can I help you?"

"Uh," I clear my throat not sure where to begin. I've never been one to ask for help. "I, um, was, um, wondering what I needed to do to see a therapist." I finally squeeze out through my dry throat.

"Yes, of course," the woman responds. She goes through the process in great detail, and after fifteen minutes, I have my first appointment scheduled for Thursday morning.

I hang up the phone, slipping it in my pocket and look around the once again dark room. I can barely see anything, and yet images dance around me, fuzzy shapes and figures that won't seem to leave me alone no matter how bad I want them too.

I sigh and close my eyes. What the hell am I going to do? I need to get out of this room. I'm losing my fucking mind even more than I already have.

I push myself up out off the couch that I haven't left since London was in here and find some shoes to slip on.

A few minutes later, I find myself heading towards Main

Street. I don't know where I plan to go or what I plan to do, but the glow of the sun beginning to set feels nice on my back and the salty ocean breeze wakes me up.

Maybe I needed this more than I realized.

I continue to walk down the sidewalk, stopping just short of a bright flashing neon sign that screams at me to go in. I glance up at the building where large white script shines against the aged brick - Jason's Bar. It's nothing fancy, that's for sure, but it looks like the perfect place to sulk.

I swing the door open, stepping inside. My eyes slowly adjust to the dim lighting. The bar is small and a bit dusty, but that doesn't seem to slow business down. Groups of people stand around tall, metal bar top tables strategically placed around the perimeter of the room, while others use the center of the floor as a makeshift dance floor. Loud country music fills the room, and a crowd of people line dance in the middle.

My body and mind begin to relax in the calming atmosphere, almost as if the chill state of everyone around me is seeping in through my skin. Something about this place just feels familiar and safe.

I sidle up to the bar, claiming a stool next to two men, and order a nice cold beer. Normally, I'd drink whiskey, but tonight I need something different.

The cold ale slides down my throat easily.

"That's a local one right there," the red-headed man says next to me, pointing at my beer.

"Is it? It's really good," I respond, taking another sip.

"Sure is. Made down in Charleston at an old cotton factory that was turned into a brewery a few years back. Best stuff around."

I nod, still not in the mood to talk, especially not to strangers. He seems to take the hint and turns back to his friend.

I drain the rest of the bottle and order a second one, sipping on it a little slower this time.

To avoid any more strangers trying to talk to me, I pull my phone out of my pocket. I don't know what I plan to do with it. I don't have social media and the only person I want to hear from I know won't text me back.

That doesn't stop me from clicking on her name or staring at the message I sent her and read a thousand times already.

I don't know what my problem is or why I can't seem to stop thinking about her. My mind seems to only have two thought processes lately - the accident or London. And there's no way to satisfy both of them at the same time.

Doesn't seem to keep me from trying though.

London takes my mind off the guilt but drowning in it is what I deserve.

It's just not what I want. I don't want to relive that night 24/7, hence me finally calling a counselor.

But if I don't relive the moment, how else am I supposed to punish myself?

I slam my now empty bottle of beer down on the counter, the ringing it makes as it connects singing over the loud music. I lay a twenty on the counter next to it and head outside, my phone in my hand and ready to call London.

Before I can talk myself out of it, the phone is ringing, and it's too late to hang up now. It rings for what feels like forever. I'm starting to think she's not going to answer when I hear the melodic tone of her voice across the line. Everything in my body responds, jolting me with a need I could have sworn didn't exist anymore.

"Hey," she greets cautiously.

It's a simple response, a typical greeting, and yet, it brings me quickly to attention.

"Hey, sorry, I don't really know why I called you," I explain nervously, rubbing the back of my neck and feeling something completely foreign to me.

"Brayden, why don't you go play some video games for a bit?" she suggests, her voice muffled from what I imagine is her hand covering the speaker.

I groan. What am I doing? I'm interrupting her night for … for what?

"Sorry about that," she mumbles, clearly focused on the phone call again.

I wince. She shouldn't be the one apologizing. "No, it's fine. If you're busy, I can let you go."

It's a sorry excuse, but I need to let this go. I need to break this connection between us somehow.

But shit. I don't want to. Is it so wrong that I want to know her better, to taste those soft lips again?

I'm so fucked up, and I know I have to stop this. I'm drowning in a sea of regret. I don't know what I want anymore, and I don't know how to make it out of these waves. I keep moving, keep fighting, but it feels pointless against the strength of it all.

"You don't have to let me go," she whispers, pulling me back out of my insane thoughts.

"You sure?" I ask, unsure of everything, especially myself.

"Yea," she pauses. "What are you up to?"

I sigh with relief. Mundane conversation is just what I need. "Just walking through town. Figured I needed some new scenery."

She chuckles lightly. "I'd imagine so. I bet that hotel room needed a change of scenery as well."

I shake my head and let myself smile at the way she pokes fun at me just like we're old friends. "I'm sure it did."

"You should check out Jason's Bar while you're out or you could go down to the pier. They're doing some night fishing thing tonight, I think. Do you fish?" She's rambling, and I'm grateful. I can tell she's not sure what we're supposed to be talking about, and maybe she's a little nervous too.

"No, I don't fish," I say, letting her light voice take away the dark pain for a little while.

"I don't fish either. Never could get past taking them off the hook or even putting the worms on the hook for that matter. Way too gross for me."

"Yea, that part doesn't bother me. It's the sitting and waiting that's the hard part."

"Nah, that's the best part," she argues. "Just you, your thoughts, and the fish, of course."

"Of course," I agree, slightly sarcastic.

Silence fills the line between us. It's not awkward, but comfortable, like two old friends just enjoying the time with each other.

"Jamie," her soft voice breaks the silence. "Why'd you really call tonight?" she asks, cautiously.

"I don't know," I whisper. "I guess I just needed to hear a friendly voice, and I wanted to tell you that I called that therapist."

"Oh, right, that's good," she says, her voice dropping just a bit. "Well, I need to go put Brayden to bed, but I'll see ya around."

I can tell she expected me to say something else, something about the kiss. Her voice is no longer soft and hopeful; instead, it's melancholic. I can't help the urge to instantly make her smile or laugh or anything to hear her light, happy voice again.

She doesn't give me the chance before she hangs up, and I suppose I deserve that.

Eleven

London

Confused.

I'm so freaking confused.

Kiss.

Text.

Call.

Everything he does is a contradiction, and I don't know what the hell to do about it. It's been almost a week since that phone call and no word from him. Nada. Zip. Zilch. Nothing.

I want to call him on his bullshit, but I'm not sure it would even matter if I did. Hell, I'm not even sure he knows what he's doing. Based on his random and erratic actions, I'd say he's just as confused as I am.

Which is annoying as hell.

I'm a grown ass woman with a child and a full-time job. I don't have time for whatever this is -- if it's even a *thing* to begin with.

Shit, now I'm thinking in riddles and confusing myself even more.

I shuffle some papers on my desk, then decide to walk out into the lobby. My body is way too jittery and antsy right now to be sitting down.

Clearly, I'm not the only one, I think as my eyes find Jamie pacing through the lobby.

How is it even possible that a man I barely know could have me this messed up and confused already? I mean, it's been, what, a week? Maybe two. There's absolutely no reason for me to...

His eyes meet mine, and damn if the look he gives me doesn't make me go weak in the knees. I'm clearly a walking cliche with the way he affects me.

There's a mixture of pain and torture, combined with hunger and an ounce of hope in his dark eyes. I question the tortured look and the meaning behind it. Maybe I should have read those tabloid articles. At least, I'd have some clue as to what's going on in that head of his.

I take a step towards him, and he does the same until we're

inches apart. "How are you doing today?" I ask, fighting the urge to reach for him and comfort him again.

"I…" he pauses, shaking his head. "Fuck this," he growls, grabbing my face and touching his lips to mine.

Instantly, I forget where I am and what I should be doing. I open my lips for him, and our tongues meet, clashing together like opposite personalities.

Our kiss is so heated, the need so strong that we can't seem to get enough. I feel the heat deep within my core as my pulse quickens, our mouths fighting for that connection.

He pulls back first, panting and placing his forehead on mine. "Fuck," he mutters in between breaths.

"Mhm," I agree, not quite able to form any words as my mind still processes the feelings that kiss ignited.

I don't know where the hell that came from or why he kissed me again, but I don't care because that kiss was a million times hotter than the one before.

"I don't deserve you. I can't have you, and yet I can't seem to stay away from you," he confesses with a whisper.

"What do you mean? Why do you keep saying you don't deserve me?" I ask, desperately needing to know.

"There's something, I don't know what it is, that keeps bringing my mind back to you. But I'm fucked up, London, so fucked up."

The way he says those words and looks at me with his

piercing gaze of pain makes my heart cry out for him. I can hear the brokenness in his words, and I want to put those pieces back together, to learn the real Jamie.

"We're all a little fucked up," I say, trying to rationalize this for him.

He shakes his head and steps back from me. I search the lobby for anyone watching. Thankfully, no one's in here.

He spins away from me, facing the decorative fireplace that sits in the middle of the far wall.

"It's not like that," he insists. "There's so much more to it than that. I just…I don't know if I can be what you need." His voice is somehow even more tortured than before, twisting my heart into knots, but also pissing me off. What does he know about what I need? We barely know each other.

"Who says I need anything? Up until you kissed me, we've only ever been friendly with each other. I mean, we're strangers."

He waves me off. "Never mind. This was stupid. I don't know what I was thinking."

"No," I say a little louder than necessary and stomp my foot like a little girl. "You do not get to keep doing this. You do *not* get to keep giving me crazy ass mixed signals here. I know we don't know each other well, but even you can't deny whatever keeps bringing us together. I can't explain this connection to a complete stranger, but it's there, and this," I motion between us, "can't keep happening. You either want to get to know me or you don't, but you can't have it both ways. And you sure as hell can't have the benefits just because, not that I wouldn't mind doing it a thousand more times. And this 'you deserve better' shit is nonsense. The only one who gets to decide what I deserve is me."

I'm rambling. My thoughts are spewing out of my mouth faster than I have the chance to think them through. And Jamie still isn't looking at me, but that's fine. I just wish I could read his expression, tell what he's thinking after the word vomit that just flew from my mouth. It seems to be the only way for me to know what he's really feeling; that much I've learned in this short amount of time.

My cheeks are hot and I'm sweating from the fire within me as silence fills the room around us. When he doesn't make a move to say anything, I decide to break the silence.

"I never asked you for anything," I sigh. "You're the one who kissed me first - both times. All I've ever tried to be is your friend. Do with that what you will, but please stop confusing the hell out of me with this, 'I can't have you, but I can't stay away from you,' bullshit."

He turns to me, nodding. "You're right. I did do that, and I'm sorry. I don't know what I'm doing anymore."

I smile, lightening the mood a smidge. "So you keep saying."

I plop down on my couch, groaning. What did I do? I ruined what could have potentially been the best time of my life.

I close my eyes and Jamie's face appears, a sexy smirk

floating across the inside of my eyelids.

What the hell is wrong with me? Why do I always want the things I can't have? I mean this is how I ended up stuck in Sunrise with an eight-year-old son. I wanted something I couldn't have.

The only difference is that I got it for a few months, and then he was gone.

Well, he wasn't gone just like that, but he left me pretty high and dry for another, better-looking, summer fling. Good ole Hamish. He was the hottest guest to ever step foot in the hotel, or at least that's what my eighteen-year-old self thought.

I don't know why I ever imagined he'd want anything more than sex from me, but that didn't stop me from running to him when I found out I was pregnant. What did stop me was his response to me when I told him.

"I don't want anything to do with that bastard child or his whore of a mother," he'd said. It's like he wasn't even talking to me, but to someone else. The words bothered me, but it was the disgusted look on his face that really got to me.

That's when I vowed I'd never date another guest staying at the hotel.

Obviously, I know that not every guest is like Hamish, but it was awkward as hell when we'd run into each other after that. And I never wanted to feel like I was the dirt on someone's shoes again.

Of course, as the manager now, that feeling is a little different, but it's still there.

Not around Jamie though.

He's not once made me feel less than him. Maybe that's why I can't seem to get him out of my head or can't seem to remember why I made the rule in the first place?

There's just something I can't quite put my finger on. Something that pulls me to him even though I know it's a bad idea and even though I know he's so messed up. I don't need that in my life. Yet, I can't deny the need to be near him, to help him find his way out of the brokenness.

My phone pings with a text from Sabrina.

S: Hey girl, what are you up to?

Me: Not much just wondering why I'm so stupid.

S: ??

Me: Hot movie star, incredible make out session, and my dumb ass.

S: Yea, I'm gonna need more details than that. Tomorrow night? My place? Girl's night?

Me: Sounds perfect.

I lean my head back against the couch and sigh. Maybe time with my best friend can put this into perspective for me.

Twelve
Jamie

I haven't seen or talked to London in 24 hours, and it's been almost torturous for me. I don't know why, as she made it clear yesterday that we don't even know each other, but maybe that's the problem.

No matter how much I shouldn't, I want to get to know her, to spend time with her. I can't seem to make myself stop thinking about her or the passion in her kiss.

I shake my head, forcing her sexy body and soft lips from my mind. I can't do this with her. I'll only hurt her. It's just who I am. If I can hurt that innocent little girl, what else am I capable of doing?

Even if it was an accident, I can't stop those questions from flying around my mind.

I'm broken, shattered into a thousand pieces. I don't know how to let myself be happy, to let go of the guilt, but London makes me want to figure it out. When I'm talking to her, I remember what life used to feel like. I forget that my life was turned upside down, and I forget just how broken I am.

Yet, as much as I want to let it go and move on, the need to never forget is stronger. That's why a part of me was relieved when London said she couldn't keep doing this. Even though it felt wrong, I know I need to step back from whatever this is, especially after my first therapy appointment this morning. It wasn't as bad as I thought it would be, and while I still feel completely fucked up, I think talking about this with a professional could actually help.

This morning was all about talking through what happened, how I feel about it, and my responses to the trauma. The therapist told me that this will be a long process, but it's something I can come back from. I set up reoccurring appointments this morning for twice a week. Even if she can't put my broken pieces back together, simply talking about it this morning helped take a little bit of the weight off my shoulders.

I have no doubt this will take time though. I'm carrying around far too much baggage.

I shake these thoughts from my head. I need to stop thinking about this. I need to … I don't know… but sitting here replaying the feel of London's lips on mine or analyzing the unexplainable need to be around her or thinking about how damaged I am won't help anything. It won't change the facts.

I pick up my phone and dial Damon's number. He's the only friend I have, sadly, that's what fame and fortune does. You can't trust anyone, and when you do, it always bites you in the ass. Damon's been the one and only person in Hollywood that's stuck by my side through everything.

"Hey, man, what's up?" he answers cheerily, which is unusual for his hard, businessman persona.

"You sound happy?" I note, a hint of a smile on my lips.

"Just been a good day."

"Good."

The line is silent as I process what I want to tell him. I know I called him, but now I'm second guessing what I want to say to him. He's been suggesting that I see a counselor for months, but it wasn't until London suggested it as well that I did. I don't know how he'll respond when I tell him.

"Jamie? You still there?" he asks, and I can hear him shifting around in his chair.

"Yea, I'm here," I mutter.

"Well, you called me, so what did you need?"

"Hell, I don't know. Just didn't want to be alone with my thoughts anymore."

"That's a nice surprise. Lately, all you've wanted to do is be alone with your thoughts. I mean, that *is* why you didn't answer me the seven hundred times I called the other day."

"Yea, sorry about that."

I hate that that's the person I've become, the person who hides in the dark, ignoring everyone around them, but sometimes, I just don't have the energy to deal with them.

"I know, and it's okay. Was there something you wanted to talk to me about?"

"Not really," I say, leaning back against the cushions of the couch and rubbing my temples. It's a lie. I do want to talk to him about London, therapy, and the fact that I'm finally starting to feel things other than guilt and agony. I'm just not sure I want to hear his thoughts on it.

"That's a bunch of bullshit. You wouldn't have called me unless there was something you wanted to tell me." His voice is hard as he calls me out.

"You're right, but I'm not sure I want to know what you think about it."

"What if I promise not to make any comments about what you say?"

I choke out a fake laugh. "Right, like you could keep your mouth shut."

"Promise," he states, and I imagine him holding up three fingers for scout's honor, even though he was definitely no Boy Scout.

"I took your advice. I saw a counselor. Actually, had my first appointment this morning," I admit.

"You did?" I hear the curiosity in his voice. I wait patiently for him to say some smart-ass comment about how it's time I finally listened to him, but it never comes.

"Yea, I did. I still feel so fucked up but letting it all out today helped lift some of the heaviness."

"That's really great, man. I'm glad you're talking to someone." His words are genuine, and there's nothing snarky or sarcastic about them.

Silence fills the line between us once again as I debate whether or not to bring up London.

The words fall out before I can stop them. "I met a girl here. Well, actually, she's very much a woman."

"Wait, what?"

"I know. It's the last thing I expected, but I haven't been able to get her out of my head, and I know that's fucking crazy because I don't know her at all. I just can't explain it."

"Man, that's fucking great. Therapy and a girl, maybe there's hope for you after all." And there's the comment I've been waiting on.

"No, it's not," I argue. "And it's not great because she's such a sweet person, and I can't give her anything because I'm a broken piece of shit." Somehow saying it out loud makes me feel even worse. I am a broken piece of shit, so why do I keep finding myself with

London?

"Jamie," Damon says sternly. I imagine him shaking his head and frowning as well. "You're a mess. I get that, but you can't stop living your life. I'm sure your therapist would tell you the same thing. Whether you like it or not, you're still alive and at some point, you're going to have to accept that."

"You're right. I am a mess, and that's exactly why I've stopped living my life. I deserve it. I deserve to be miserable and unhappy for the rest of my life," I practically yell at him. My body is shaking and I'm fuming inside.

"That's the thing. You don't deserve it, but I'm clearly not going to convince you otherwise. Maybe the counselor finally can." His words sound harsh, but I know he doesn't mean what he says. He's irritated and frustrated with having the same conversation with me over and over again.

I can't blame him for it. If it were me on his side, I'd probably do the same. But I'm not him.

"I have a meeting I need to prepare for," his sharp voice cuts through the phone, and he's no longer in best friend mode. "I can only hope this trip and the therapy sessions help you find your desire to live again, because this Jamie sucks balls."

The call clicks off, and I'm left with his words bouncing off the corners of my mind and echoing through the room like a pinball machine.

I lay my phone down on the table in front of me, desperately hoping that therapy is the key to saving me from the drowning waters I seem to be stuck in. Damon and London seem to think so.

London, sweet, genuine London. She's a complete stranger who leads with her heart, and I want her to be in my life so bad. I want to see her kind smile every minute of every day because something about that smile warms me on the inside, melts away bits and pieces of the icy man I've become.

I know I'm messed up. I know I need to figure my shit out, but I don't want to stay away from her while I do it. I need her to be a part of this journey with me because honestly, I'm not sure I can face my demons without someone willing me to.

My phone lights up with an incoming text. I pick it up, seeing London's name flash across the screen.

L: Hey, just checking in. Wanted to make sure you're okay.

Me: I'm fine, thanks.

L: Good.

I wait to see if she's going to send anything else, but she doesn't. And I mean, what else should I expect from a virtual stranger? Except she doesn't feel like a stranger anymore. Not when she's the reason I walked into a counselor's office this morning. Damon hounded me for months about it, but one phone number from her had me sitting across from the one person I never thought I would - a therapist.

Thirteen

London

I don't know why I sent that text. In fact, it's completely beyond me. I just felt like I should check on him, make sure he was doing okay after everything. I know he doesn't have anyone here, just me. It's the least I could do as his friend.

Well, that's what I keep telling myself as I stand in front of Sabrina's apartment, knocking softly and waiting for her to open the door.

"Let yourself in. Door's open," I hear her yell from the other side of the white metal-plated door.

You wouldn't think Sunrise would be big enough to have an

apartment complex, but there is a surprisingly large amount of people that move here and commute into Charleston for work.

I swing open the door. "Yoo hoo, honey, I'm home," I holler in a high-pitched, sing-song voice.

Sabrina laughs. "In the kitchen, darlin'."

I slip my shoes off and head down the short hallway into her kitchen. "Where's Ki?" I ask, climbing on the cold, hard, metal bar stool at the island. My butt hits the hard frame and I cringe. "You really need some padding for these stools. They're so damn uncomfortable."

"I know," she chuckles as she fights with the cork in the wine bottle in her hand. "I keep telling my sister, Reese, that, but she's all 'I'm too busy saving lives' to care. To be fair though, she's hardly ever here. Oh, and speaking of being too busy to care, that was Ki's excuse for not showing up tonight," she says, finally popping the cork from the wine bottle. "Her loss though."

"Is it really though? I mean she's probably 'busy' with that hunk of a boyfriend she has now," I wink.

Sabrina shudders. "Ew, was it really necessary to put that image in my head? Now I'm thinking about the two of them getting it on, and that's just so wrong, especially since I've known them my whole life." She sticks her tongue out with disgust.

"Sorry."

"No, you're not." She places a glass of white wine in front of me.

I look at her over the glass, quirking my brows. "We're drinking white tonight? I didn't think you liked white wine?"

Sabrina can be crazy, spontaneous, and blunt, but with wine, she's always predictable. It's red wine or no wine. It's the one thing about her you can almost always be sure of, except for tonight.

"I needed something different," she explains, shrugging her shoulders like it's no big deal and sipping on her wine.

"I guess I can understand that." Except I don't understand the sudden change at all.

She sets her glass on the counter and opens the fridge, pulling a board of meats and cheeses out. My eyes open wide. "A charcuterie board? Who are you and what did you do with Sabrina?" I gasp.

She puts the board on the island bar and firmly places her hands on her hips. "Your sarcasm is not necessary. I know it's shocking, but I do enjoy more than red wine, cake, and greasy foods."

I tilt my head to the side and eye her skeptically. "There are plenty of areas in your life where I expect you to change things at least three times a week, but there are two things that never change - the alcohol you drink and the food you eat. Now, here you are being all sophisticated."

She rolls her eyes. "Don't you think you're being a little dramatic? Ya know I like to try new things, and that's exactly what I'm doing."

"Yea, sure," I say, still skeptical.

She climbs up onto the stool next to me and cringes. "You're right. I do need some padding for these things."

"Well, duh, if my fat ass doesn't like them, then you know you need some padding."

She grabs a cracker, some meat, and cheese, making a sandwich. She doesn't look at me when she speaks, but I can hear the frown in her tone. "You are not fat. You look damn hot. And if I were into girls, I'd totally be into you."

I chuckle, creating my own little cracker sandwich. "Well, thanks."

"You're welcome," she winks.

We just sit there awhile, eating, drinking, and gossiping. Soon enough, the charcuterie board is empty, with the exception of a few cracker crumbs, and our wine glasses need a refill.

"I don't know about you, but I'm about to refill this glass and take my butt to the nice comfy couch over there." She points to the living room that's only separated from the kitchen by the couch.

"That sounds like an excellent idea," I say, standing and feeling the numbness prickling my back side. Can butts fall asleep? Apparently so.

I walk around the counter, stretching the muscles in my booty as I go. Sabrina hands me the bottle and I refill my glass.

"So, tell me about this guy you mentioned in your text last night," she starts as she plops down onto the couch, giving me a smirk. "And don't leave out all the good details."

"There are no good details."

"Liar," Sabrina accuses, pointing a finger at me as I curl up on the opposite side of the couch.

I laugh, a blush creeping to my cheeks and giving away the truth.

"So, I met a guy at work, but he's not just any guy. He's Jameson Decker, the actor," I confess, staring at my glass of wine and rubbing my finger around the rim absentmindedly.

"As in the hottest actor in Hollywood?"

I nod, glancing up to see her mouth hanging open and her eyes wide.

"The movie star that your son is obsessed with?"

I nod again.

"Wow," she says. "What's he like?" Her eyes are dreamy, and a pang of jealousy pierces my heart.

My heart flutters in my chest as I think about how to describe him. Perfect. Wonderful. Broken. Not what I expected at all.

"He's gorgeous, and he has muscles that are perfection," I settle on.

She eyes me curiously. "And you know this from experience or from stalking him on the internet?"

"They peek through his shirt, like you can see the creases of his muscles because his shirts are so tight."

"Uh-huh," she nods, her eyes telling me she doesn't believe a word I'm saying. "And how does he kiss?"

My cheeks heat, and I take a large gulp of wine. "Pretty

freaking incredible," I mutter shyly.

I'm not nearly as open about this stuff as Sabrina. I like to keep the personal parts of my life personal, but not her. She loves to talk about it, and for once, a part of me kind of wants to talk about it, too.

"Aw, that's so adorable," she squeals.

I roll my eyes. "But it's not going to happen again," I say, draining the rest of my wine.

I go to stand, but Sabrina stops me. "Nope, wine can wait; you need to explain right now."

I sit back down and look at Sabrina before sinking back into the couch. I sigh, closing my eyes and formulating my words. "There's more going on than meets the eye."

"What do you mean?"

"The other day, his manager called the hotel because he wasn't answering his phone. I went to check on him and found him sulking in the dark. Then, yesterday, he tells me he's fucked up and can't give me what I need, which, by the way, I have no clue what that means."

"What do you think about all of it?" Sabrina asks, and it's a really good question - one I don't have an answer to.

"I don't know. I want to help him because I feel this unexplainable connection to him, but I don't know if it's worth my energy. Besides, I don't even know what has him so messed up. What if it's the accident I remember seeing something about a few months ago? What if something really bad happened? Do I want to get involved in it? I mean I don't just have myself to think about."

She nods, setting her glass down on the end table and leaning forward. "Yea, it's not as easy for you to do things like that as it is for me. However, I will say this. That connection you're talking about doesn't happen often, which means you should fight for it when it does. There are a lot of things you need to think about, and I understand that, but the best things don't come easily."

A lone tear slides down my cheek, and I can't say why I'm crying. Maybe it's because she makes so much sense? Or maybe it's the way she spoke, so full of emotion and soul? Either way, I have a decision to make.

"Look, it's easy to choose the safe route, but it's not nearly as fun or rewarding. If it were me, I'd be sticking myself into every part of his life until the walls come crashing down and he lets himself start to heal. But we also know I have terrible luck with men, so." She shrugs her shoulders.

I don't know how to respond because I don't know what I'm going to do. Ki's words from the other day float into my mind. She'd said a similar thing then as well. Find a way to spend as much time with him as possible, but with the blatantly obvious sexual tension between us, is that really a smart idea?

Fourteen

Jamie

For someone who doesn't want to be happy and has decided they can't have a relationship because of that, I certainly spend a lot of time hoping to catch a glimpse of London or run into her. Anything to spend some kind of time with the woman who's somehow nestled her way into my life, even though I know I'll only hurt her.

That's why I'm here in the local park, wandering along the trail and enjoying the scent of lilies and wildflowers. I went looking for London today in the lobby. The young girl that works there noticed me looking for something. She didn't even have to ask, apparently, because she immediately said that London wasn't in today, but then she'd mentioned London taking her son to the park for the day.

I didn't need to hear anymore. I went straight out the front doors without a second thought and ended up in the park, hoping she'd be here and that I might run into her.

So far, no luck, but I needed the fresh air anyway, especially since I've been spending so much time inside. That's the problem with not knowing anyone and not working. I have zero things to occupy my time, besides therapy. As much as it's helping me deal with the accident, it's rehashing the past so much that being alone is too much for me sometimes. I think that's why I keep finding myself searching for London.

I've never met a woman quite like her, and definitely not one who captured my attention in under ten minutes. I'm usually far too cautious to allow myself the pleasure, but I can't help it with her. There's just something about the warmth in her smile and the genuineness to her voice that makes me think she's worth it to break my promise to myself.

The sound of laughter rings through the air. I round the corner of the path, my eyes landing on a familiar face, and my heart does a weird extra beat.

I stop just short of them playing catch. Brayden tosses the ball and London barely catches it. They laugh as she lobs it back to Brayden. He catches the ball effortlessly, and a wide grin spreads across his face.

"Mr. Jamie," he yells, dropping the ball and rushing towards me.

He stops a few feet in front of me, London lagging a little further behind.

"Hey there, kiddo," I say, rustling my hand in his hair. "What are you guys doing out here today?"

"We're playing catch." He holds up his glove. "You wanna play with me?" he asks, enthusiastically.

My heart leaps into my throat, and I can't think of anything I want to do more at this moment. I open my mouth to speak, but London cuts me off. "B, I'm sure he's busy." She places her hand on his shoulder, avoiding my gaze.

"Actually, I'd love to play catch. It's been a while, but I think I've still got it," I respond, my intense gaze on London's face. I don't miss the flick of lusty fire in her eyes as I look at her, and I can't express in words what that does to me. If Brayden weren't here, I'd probably have her in my arms right now.

She slips the glove off her hand and tosses it at me, not looking at me as she does, but I know what she's thinking from the tint of pink on her cheeks that wasn't there a few minutes ago. "Well, then, here ya go," she says.

We all walk back towards where they were playing catch, London stepping off to the side. "What are you going to do?" I ask.

"Sit and watch, which I prefer much more than actually playing," she explains self-deprecatingly, dropping to the grass a few yards away.

"Not a sports person?"

She shakes her head swiftly. "Not even close, but Brayden loves sports, so I try."

I feel a warmth spread through my veins. I admire the way she clearly loves her son, and at the same time, it also makes my gut twist. Is this the way that family loved their daughter? Enough to do the things she loved even if they didn't?

As if Brayden can sense I'm going into a dark place, he hollers, "Come on, Mr. Jamie. Let's play."

I shake off the feelings the best I can, forcing myself to live in the moment. I walk over to where he stands. "Where do you want me?"

"Scoot back some," he directs, flicking his hand back and forth.

I take a few steps back, and he tosses the ball in my direction. I catch the ball with ease. "Good arm," I compliment loudly.

His face lightens up. "Thanks, I practice a lot, so I can be the best. I want to play with the Red Sox one day."

"Why the Red Sox?"

"Because I love red socks, and they're such an awesome team."

I nod, chuckling, and pass the ball back to him with a little less strength than I'd normally use. It starts to fall just in front of him, and he moves quickly, placing his glove just underneath the ball and catching it.

"That's quite a big dream. You have to work really hard to make it that far in baseball."

"Yea, I know. Mom keeps telling me that I have to practice a lot, listen to my coaches, and want it more than anything for it to happen, which I do," he states, throwing the ball back to me.

"She's right. You will have to do all those things and more, but I have no doubt you can make it happen."

"Really?" he asks, excitedly catching the ball I just returned to him. He stops, holding the ball in his hand.

"Yes, really, if the rest of your game is anything like your throw, you must be a good ball player, and you have passion and determination. Those two things are the most important things you need to make your dreams happen."

He tilts his head to the side, thinking about what I said. He crinkles his eyebrows. "Is that what you needed to be an actor?"

I nod. "Pretty much. You can do anything you want to as long as you work hard to make it happen."

His eyes shine bright with hope, and my heart beats a little faster and livelier. My chest feels warm again, and it's a feeling I haven't gotten in so long.

I don't have time to analyze it though. Brayden throws the ball to me before I have a chance to think about it any further.

For the next hour, we chat about his favorite things: food, baseball, and video games, as we toss the ball back and forth. I let the release of energy take over my mind and focus only on the task at hand. It's a nice feeling to not have my thoughts taking over my brain like usual.

"I need some water," Brayden exclaims, his face red and sweaty.

"Me too," I agree, following him over to where his mom sits.

She opens a cooler I hadn't even realized was there earlier and hands us both a bottle of water.

"Thanks," I say, taking it graciously from her and unscrewing the lid. I chug half the bottle in one go, noticing Brayden do the same.

"Y'all were thirsty," London notes, leaning back on the grass with her hands holding her up.

I take a seat next to her. "Well, yea, it's hotter than blue blazes out here. And unlike some people, we were actually exerting ourselves."

"Excuse me," she protests, her mouth hanging open in mock offense. "I did plenty of exercise before you showed up." Her mouth closes and turns into a pout.

"No, you didn't, Mom. We'd only been playing for like ten minutes," Brayden blurts out.

"Brayden," she squeals, slapping him on the arm.

I chuckle. My feet thank me for giving them a break as they throb from standing so long. "I think your son might have something against you. He always seems to be calling you on your BS."

She glares at me, then Brayden. "If he knows what's good for him, he'll stop doing it," she growls.

"But you told me not to lie. You said it's a bad thing to do and people can get hurt."

London's cheeks blush. "Not the point," she argues.

"Sounds exactly like the point," I say, lifting an accusing brow at her.

"No one asked you," she waves me off.

I can't help the laughter that spills from my mouth. She looks like an angry, attitude-filled child, and it's just so damn cute.

My eyes land on her pouting lips and the sudden desire to kiss her hits me hard in the chest. What is it about her that makes me want her more than I've ever wanted anyone else?

Fifteen

London

My cheeks burn. Jamie's intense stare heats my body and creates a need inside me that's becoming increasingly common when I'm around him. He studies my lips, and I don't miss the hunger that flashes in them. For someone who keeps telling me he can't do this, he certainly seems to forget that himself.

I look away, hoping if I can't see the heat in his eyes, it will tamper down the fire building within me. It doesn't work though. His gaze burns my skin more than the sun on this hot day.

I have no doubt that if Brayden weren't sitting here with us, his lips would be on mine, his body on top of me, showing me just how much he wants me. And I'd let him, too, especially after watching him play catch with my son. I can't even begin to describe the way my heart fluttered in my chest at the sight.

I glance at Brayden, but he seems to be oblivious to the fire burning between Jamie and I. Thank the good Lord above.

"Mr. Jamie," Brayden says. "What are you doing tonight?"

My brows furrow, and I rack my brain for why my son is asking Jamie about his plans.

"Not sure yet," Jamie answers, glancing at me.

I shrug my shoulders. "Beats me," I mouth to him.

"Do you want to come over for dinner?" he asks.

I hold my breath. My heart stops, my palms sweat, and my throat goes dry. My son did not just invite Jamie to our house for dinner. There's no possible way.

Jamie looks over at me, a hint of amusement bouncing in his eyes, and his lips twitch.

Please say no. Please say no. I beg in my mind, hoping this special connection we have helps him read my thoughts.

"Sure, I'd love that," he says, flashing a smirk my way.

What good is this stupid connection if it doesn't allow us to read each other's minds? Unless that smirk meant he could, and he just ignored my mental plea.

What do I do now? I can't very well unextend the invite. It's rude and would crush Brayden.

"Yes!" Brayden's excitement makes me cringe. Nothing good

can come from having Jamie over for dinner. Absolutely nothing.

So, maybe it's not so bad. Jamie and Brayden play card games at the table, chatting about various things while I prepare dinner. It's nothing fancy, just some fried chicken and mashed potatoes, but it's a Southern classic that Brayden loves.

I turn the burners on the stove off, plating the fried chicken and potatoes. I pour the gravy I also made into a little bowl and pull out some silverware.

"Dinner's ready," I announce, stepping back from the counter where the plates sit.

Brayden jumps up from the table and runs over to the counter. He grabs a plate and silverware and pours a spoonful of gravy on top of everything on his plate. "It smells delicious, Mom," he says, his stomach growling loudly.

"Thanks, B." I laugh, watching him walk back to the table carefully. He has a tendency to move quickly all the time which has led to several dinners splattered across my floor over the years.

Jamie sidles up next to me at the counter, leaning in so close I can feel his breath on my ear and whispers, "It looks delicious. I can't wait to taste it."

I shiver. The way he says those words, I know he isn't referring to the food.

He smirks, grabs his plate, and heads to the table, sitting down across from Brayden.

I don't move, my body still reeling from what I'm pretty sure was him telling me he couldn't wait to taste me. My legs clench together and heat pools in my stomach. He's doing it again, giving me all these mixed signals, and I don't know what to do with it.

I hear Sabrina in the back of my mind, and I decide to just go with the flow. Our chemistry is undeniable, and I deserve to have some fun.

Even if it might crush my heart in the end.

I grab my plate and drizzle gravy on top of everything. One thing my Southern heritage taught me was that gravy goes with every meal. You just need to have the right kind of gravy to make it work. You need a thicker gravy for biscuits and a thinner one for meats, and so on.

I take a seat at the small, four-person table. I'm nestled between Jamie and Brayden, but my chair is slightly closer to Jamie. I swear I can feel the heat from his body, or maybe it's from his gaze. Either way, it's intoxicating and confusing all at the same time.

We eat in silence, me trying to ignore the fact that this incredibly delicious man is sitting next to me. It doesn't work though. My body senses his every movement and reacts in a way I wasn't sure was possible. I'm glad I chose to say screw it because I don't think being just friends is a possibility, not when I can cut the sexual tension in this room with a knife.

When dinner is over, the boys clean up the table and bring them to me to rinse and place in the dishwasher. Brayden disappears within seconds, quickly losing interest in helping to clean up.

Jamie hands me the last of the dishes. "Thank you," I say, taking them from him. "You didn't have to help clean up."

"Sure, I did. You cooked. The least I could do is help clean up." His smile could knock me to my knees if I let it. Thankfully, the counter holds me up.

"It's nice to know some men still have manners," I comment, closing the dishwasher and turning it on.

"Well, I have them most of the time." He smirks, leaning against the counter and reminding me of all those bad boys in the 80's movies I used to watch growing up.

I fight the urge to fan myself, because damn does he have me all hot and bothered right now.

I knew tonight wasn't a good idea. I can't seem to control my reactions to him, and I definitely don't need my son witnessing this tension. I don't need Brayden thinking that Jamie and I are more than just friends.

Not that he won't get that idea anyway. He always seems to be trying to find me someone to date. He may only be eight, but he's a sneaky little thing.

"Come on, let's go see what B is up to," I say, bringing up my son to remind myself we are not alone, and I cannot jump this man right here no matter how badly I want to.

"Good idea," he agrees.

Gah, what is he doing to me?

I shake my head, walking into the living room where B is centered in the middle of the couch with the TV set to Netflix.

"Good, you're done. Let's watch a movie." He yawns, pointing at the TV. He isn't going to make it through a movie, but I agree anyway.

"Okay, B, what movie do you want to watch?" I ask, sitting next to him on the couch.

Jamie stays still, looking extremely awkward.

"You going to join?" I question, noting how he rubs his hand on the back of his neck, something I've caught him doing a lot when he's nervous or uncomfortable.

"I don't want to ruin any family time."

Brayden turns around, pulling himself up to look at Jamie better. "You won't ruin anything."

Turmoil and torment fill Jamie's eyes, almost like he's fighting the urge to run out the door. Did seeing us together cause an internal battle in his mind? Why would that be?

Brayden smiles, pleading with him to join.

"Okay," he finally says, sighing. His face still holds a frown, like he doesn't really want to be here anymore.

"You don't have to stay," I say to Jamie, noticing his hesitation, and I want to offer him a way out.

"No, I want to stay," he responds and slowly takes a seat on the couch on the other side of Brayden.

I can't help but wonder if something from his past caused that hesitation. What happened tonight to change his mood in an instant? *The accident,* my mind whispers. Maybe I should read those damn tabloid articles.

I lean my head over my son as he sits slouched against his knees intent on finding a movie for us to watch. "Hey, is everything alright?" I whisper, hoping Brayden stays focused on the TV.

He nods. "It just feels like I'm intruding on something here."

I touch my fingers to his arm. "Trust me, you're not."

"If you say so," he mutters, and for a minute, I wonder if he feels like he doesn't belong here, if this is too much for him.

He doesn't say anything further, and I don't ask, not wanting to scare him off, but that doesn't drive away the curiosity floating deep within me.

Sixteen

Jamie

I take several deep breaths and move my way through the guilt drowning me. I don't know why it happens so suddenly and in such unusual circumstances. I can't seem to control it though no matter how hard I try.

The sad thing is I was doing great today. Then, I saw London and Brayden on the couch together, and something in me just snapped. All I could feel was the rush of the guilt flowing over me and the need to leave, to run out the door as fast as I could.

But Brayden's face kept me from doing any of that. He pleaded with those large puppy dog eyes for me to stay, and I couldn't find it in me to say no.

So, I stayed.

I watch mother and son as the cartoon movie about ninjas begins. Brayden is nestled into London's arms, and I find myself wishing it were me instead. The whole night has been heated like an electrical storm. Although, that's mostly my fault.

I know we discussed being friends, but I don't think I can keep fighting this attraction between us. I try. I really do. I know she deserves something more than a fling, and shit, so does her son. I'll be damned if I hurt her and her son.

The movie plays in the background, but I'm not paying attention. Instead, I find myself studying London's face, the emotions that play on them as she watches the ninja kids training. I note the way her chest moves up and down with each breath and the way her cleavage teases me.

There's nothing about her that's my typical go-to when it comes to women. She's sweet, wholesome, and crazy independent. She's nowhere near my previous girlfriends or hookups. No, she's so many levels higher than them.

That London is special, that she's unique among women, is why all of this is so hard. I want her. I want to feel her skin under me, feel myself inside her. I want to feel her shivering around me as she hits her high. And, I also want to know her, the *real* her. I want to know what made her who she is today, what her hopes and dreams are, and what motivates her.

In fact, I haven't been able to stop thinking about all the things I want to know about her.

But, to find those things out, I have to open up. I have to let myself feel something, to feel at peace with what I've done. And I'm not sure I can do that.

"Looks like you wore someone out today," London whispers, startling me back into the moment, pointing at a sleeping Brayden.

"Yea, I guess I did," I say, thinking about how much I want to wear her out.

She flicks the movie off. "I should probably get him to bed."

I stand, moving in front of her. "Here let me." I reach my hands to pick him up.

"You don't have to do that," she protests. "I can wake him up."

I shake my head. "No need to do that when I can carry him upstairs."

I lift his tiny body in my arms and pull him close. My heart clenches, and I don't know what to think about the feeling. I carry him with ease up to his room. London leads the way, flipping a light on in his baseball-themed bedroom.

"You can just lay him in the bed. I won't bother changing him. He should be alright."

I lay him in the bed and step back, letting London pull his blankets up over him and kiss him goodnight.

It's such an intimate moment and I feel so out of place.

Then, sudden panic rises in my throat, and I feel like I can't breathe. I took this from that family - moments as intimate as this with their child.

I slowly back out of the room. London quirks an eyebrow and frowns, following me into the hallway and shutting Brayden's door behind her.

"Is everything alright?" she asks softly.

I want to scream at her that it's not and never will be again. Nothing is alright. But I don't want to wake Brayden and I'm not sure I'm ready to tell her anything anyways. Instead, I just shake my head and close my eyes, trying to bring myself back to this moment and out of these depressive emotions.

I think about what the counselor said in our last session, and I slow my breathing, counting to five as I breath in and out. I feel my muscles relax and my mind slowly coming back to the here and now.

I think about London and Brayden, and everything that's good in my life at this very moment.

Slowly, I open my eyes, London's curvy frame filling my view. My eyes land on her lips, and the need to forget fills my body. I reach for London, holding my hands out to her.

She doesn't rush into my arms like I expect, though I don't know why I would expect her to. She studies me, her face asking a thousand questions I can't interpret and worry that I couldn't answer even if I knew what she was thinking. She chews on her bottom lip, thinking intently, and I harden instantly.

Finally, she moves toward me.

I wrap my arms around her, and she places her hands on my chest, looking up at me. Her blue eyes still sparkle with questions.

I won't tell her my dark secrets. Not yet.

I pull her close, staring into her eyes while she tries to read me.

She lifts her head, bringing her lips closer to mine.

I can't fight the vacuum pulling me toward her or the intensity that's been building between us all night.

Fuck this. Fuck the rules I've laid out. So, what if I can't give her my heart? Is it really that big of a deal?

Maybe it is, but who the fuck cares?

Not me.

That's definitely a lie, but I laid the cards out on the table for her. If she pushes me away, then I won't try again. But something tells me she wants this as much as I do.

My breathing picks up as I lean in towards London. Our lips connect with an explosive need. Our hunger has our tongues in a war and our hands grasping at each other.

I spin her around from Brayden's door, our mouths never losing the other's and pin her against the wall.

She moans as my hands find her waist and venture up and down her body. Our lips continue their game of tug-o'-war, pulling the other in deeper and deeper.

She whispers between kisses, "Maybe we should move this to

my room."

I lean back, breathing heavily. "Show me the way."

She takes my hand and leads me down the hallway, and I'm glad it's not right next to Brayden's room. If my plan to make her scream tonight is realized, I don't want him to be able to hear it.

We slip inside the room, and I push the door shut behind us, clicking the lock into place. My lips find hers again and my hands make quick work, slipping under her shirt and lifting it up slowly, revealing her lacy black bra.

She doesn't stop me.

She doesn't pull away from me.

She simply looks at me with a hunger in her eyes that I can relate to.

I toss her shirt to the side and reach around her back, unhooking her bra and letting it fall to the ground.

I step back, taking her half-naked self in. "Damn, you're gorgeous," I mutter, reaching for her pants. I clumsily unbutton them, then slide both her blue jeans and underwear down. "But this is even better."

She giggles, grabbing the hem of my shirt. "What about me? Don't I get to enjoy the view?" she asks, lifting it over my head and throwing it on top of her discarded clothes.

She runs her hands over my six-pack - the one I work so damn hard to maintain for my movies.

The feel of her soft fingers sends chills up my spine. She

traces my defined muscles, making me even crazier than before.

I grab her by the waist and guide her backwards toward the bed until she falls back onto it. I stand there staring at her for just a moment, enjoying the view of this amazing woman waiting for me.

"If you're worried about protection, I'm clean and on the pill," she says softly.

"That's not what I was thinking about, but that's good to know. I'm clean, too," I respond, lifting my lips into a predatory smirk.

I climb on top of her, my knees around her, trailing kisses up and down her body. I look up to see her eyes closed and a soft smile on her face. My lips continue their assault, making their way up her body to her neck.

I pause inches from her mouth. "I want all of you."

Her eyes open slowly and dreamily. "I want you too," she whispers.

"Even if this is all it is? Even if I can't ever give you more than just a fling?" I ask, needing to be sure.

"Yes," she says, breathily, her legs writhing underneath me.

"Good, because I'm about to show you just how you make me feel," I growl.

Seventeen

London

Fuck. Fuck. Fuckity fuck fuck.

I never say that word - ever but I think waking up to a movie star naked in my bed warrants it, especially when that's what we did last night.

I glance at him, his hair ruffled around his face and his gorgeous abs peeking through the sheets that he's all tangled up in.

Fuck, I think again.

What the hell did we do? I mean I know what we did, but it was so stupid and perfect and hot, and *damn*, I want to do it over and over again.

But not now, not when my son is asleep just down the hall.

Shit, what do we do when he wakes up? He's going to want to know why Jamie is still here and he'll see right through any lies I tell. He's just that dang smart.

Okay London, take a breath.

I suck in a deep breath, closing my eyes and letting my mind drift back to last night when Jamie gave me the best orgasm of my life. I've never felt such a euphoric high before, not even with my vibrator which usually does the trick.

That clearly says something about my sex life.

Boring as hell.

Not anymore, though.

No, now, I'm hooked on the one man I can't have forever.

I'm totally screwed, but in the best possible way. If I'm going to fall, which I know I will, I might as well do it while having the best sex of my life.

The clock on my nightstand flashes to a new number. Brayden will be up soon, and I have to go to work in two hours.

I glance over at the sleeping beast in my bed. He looks so peaceful while he sleeps, a big contrast to his usual tormented features. I don't want to wake him, but I have no other choice.

I nudge him with my finger, but he doesn't move. I try again, a little harder this time, but again nothing. *Damn, he's a heavy sleeper.* I try one last time, using the full force of my hand on his chest.

"Damn, woman, what is your problem?" he mumbles in that deep, sexy voice of his though his eyes remain closed.

"You have to get up," I say, my hand still resting on his bare chest. His muscles feel so hard and firm, and I swear my mouth waters a little bit.

He captures my arm in his hand and pulls me toward him. I go willingly, letting him wrap me up tight into his chest.

"I don't wanna go," he whispers into my ear.

"You have to," I insist, my voice muffled from his chest.

"What about round 3?"

"Round 3?"

"Yes, rounds 1 and 2 last night were fucking amazing. I can't wait to see what round 3 is like." I won't lie, hearing him say that makes my heart so happy.

I laugh, kissing his chest. "You'll have to wait for that. Brayden will be up soon, and I have to work today."

He squeezes me even tighter. "Yes! Sex at the office, even better."

I pull back from him, slapping him lightly on the chest. "Not the point of that."

"You didn't say no," he says, quirking his head to the side. I can't deny that what happened between us last night clearly affected him in a good way. I haven't seen him this way before.

"No," I say firmly, even though that's all I'm thinking about now. I won't cross that line. There's too much risk, but the thought makes me hot all the same.

He pouts with big puppy dog eyes. "How can you say no to this face?"

I'm wondering the same thing, but I don't say it. Instead, I fake it. "Easy. No! Now get up and get out of here before Brayden wakes up." I roll out of his arms and off the bed, slipping some PJ's on so I'm not still completely naked.

The last thing I need is all the questions finding us together in my normally empty bed would bring up from my son, especially the ones about boyfriends and such. Since I have no idea what last night changed between us, if anything, I do *not* want to have to try and explain it to Brayden.

Jamie groans and slides out from underneath the sheets, slipping his pants on before standing.

I can't stop myself from staring, and I'm pretty sure my mouth hangs open. I will never get used to the beauty of this man.

"Like what you see?" He smirks.

"Hell yea, I do. Now, put your shirt on and get out of my house," I demand, a teasing smile on my lips.

"Bossy much?" He slips his shirt on and gives me a quirky grin. My stomach flips and I can't help but smile back. It's nice to see him without the usual frown and brooding face. For once, I feel like I've gotten a rare glimpse of the real Jamie - the one that existed before whatever broke him.

"It's literally my job," I explain.

He strides over to me, now fully clothed. "Thank you for yesterday and last night. It was great." He leans in, giving me a soft kiss on the lips.

"You're welcome. Just to be sure, this will be happening again, right?" I quirk a brow.

He chuckles. "Fuck yea! As long as you're cool with that being all it is?" He lifts both brows, questioning me.

I don't really have much of a choice but to be okay with it; I sure as hell am not giving him up, not after last night. So, I'll take what I can get, however I can get him, and hope beyond hope that his ideas about us will change - that he'll catch feelings for me.

Like I've already done for him.

I hate to admit it to myself. I'm growing feelings for him. It's only a matter of time before I fall in love with him, but that's just how I am. I fall fast and hard.

I nod my head, letting him know I'm okay with it.

He kisses me on the forehead, then the nose, and he finally finds my lips. I open for him, deepening the kiss and enjoying one last passionate moment before he leaves.

We're all in, his hands under my shirt and mine on the rim of his pants, when there's a knock on the door and the handle jiggles.

My heart instantly beats faster. I break away from Jamie so fast. "Shit," I mutter under my breath.

"Mom, you awake? Why's the door locked?" Brayden yells through the door.

Jamie's eyes widen, and I giggle hysterically at his bugged-out look.

"You have to hide," I say, pushing him towards the closet.

"But you just said you wanted me to leave," he winks, a devilishly handsome smirk on his face.

"Yea, well, you're going to have to wait now."

"You want me to wait in your closet until when?"

"Until I get Brayden downstairs to the kitchen so you can sneak out the front door." I stare at him like he's stupid.

"How am I supposed to know when you do that?" He eyes me curiously, amusement twinkling in his eyes.

"Just get in the closet, and I'll text you when it's safe."

I feel like a teenager trying to hide a boy from her mother.

Jamie chuckles and shakes his head. His thoughts must be on the same track as mine because he says, "I haven't hidden in a girl's closet since I was sixteen."

I laugh and shove him inside. "Be quiet!"

I shut the door and walk over to the bedroom door, opening it quickly. "Sorry, B, I was changing my clothes."

He squints at me. "But you're still wearing your PJs?" he questions.

A chuckle sounds from the closet, then a bang on the floor.

"What was that?" Brayden asks, searching the room.

I grab him by the shoulders and steer him towards the hallway. "I'm sure it was just a pair of shoes falling off the shelf or something.

Come on, kid, let's go make some breakfast."

He glances over his shoulder one last time before agreeing and heading to the kitchen. Once he's seated at the table, I slip out my phone and text Jamie.

Me: Coast is clear!

J: Phew! That was a close call.

Me: Yea, no thanks to you.

J: I'm not the one who let a man stay over. ;)

Me: Shut up and get the hell out.

J: Aw, that's the sweetest thing you've ever said to me.

I roll my eyes and giggle. I could get used to this side of Jamie. I hope he continues to let me see it. Then again, it would be so much easier if he didn't because the more he shows this side of himself, the more I'll fall for him.

Eighteen
Jamie

I won't lie. That experience with London a few days ago took me back to high school and made me feel young and free again. The entire time I was with her, especially when we were alone, was the best time I've had since the accident.

I don't know what it was about that moment just before the movie that hit me so hard, but the guilt nearly crushed me. Almost like seeing London and Brayden, a little family together and happy, reminded me of everything I had stolen from that little girl's family. Surprisingly, being with London helped me get through the moment, move through the waves of emotions pulling me down, that and using the coping mechanisms I've been learning in therapy.

And the sex. Ah, it blew my fucking mind. I've had my fair share of women, but it was never anything like what it was with London.

I open the door to the Sunrise Cafe, pulling my hat low over my eyes. So far, if anyone has noticed me, they haven't said anything and I'm grateful for that.

I order a coffee and a basic breakfast sandwich and find a seat at a small, rustic table in the back of the quaint, little room. It's so bright and cheery in here with all the blues and yellows everywhere but, as much as I hate the bright colors, this cafe has some damn good coffee and food.

I slip my phone out of my pocket and check my messages. I smile when I see London's name and tap it open.

L: Morning, handsome. I've missed seeing you the last few days. Want to hang out tonight? B's at a friend's house.

This text should make my heart race and my palms sweat with nerves, but for some reason, it makes me giddy with excitement.

Me: So, that means we can have a sleepover?

L: Duh.

Me: I'll have to think about it.

L: See you at 6.

I chuckle, slipping my phone into my pocket. I like that she's so into being with me now. I wasn't sure she'd be okay with us doing … well, each other, but so far she seems cool with there being no hint of anything beyond the fling.

She hasn't been overly clingy. She hasn't expected us to hang out every day, although I'm not sure I'd mind if she did. And from what I can tell, she hasn't told the entire world, which is what usually happens.

Who can resist telling everyone they had sex with a movie star?

Apparently, London can and that makes my heart so fucking happy it's scary.

A young woman with golden hair sets my plate and coffee on the table in front of me. Her pregnant belly sticks out just under the plate. "Sorry for the wait," she says. "I'm not moving as fast in the kitchen these days."

"It's fine." I smile. "I don't have anywhere to be."

"Great," she exclaims, studying my face and making me sweat with nerves. "Do I know you?"

Shit, my heart pounds inside my chest. The last thing I need is for someone to recognize me and tell the whole damn world where I am.

I shake my head firmly. "Don't think so. I've been in here a few times before though."

She nods her head in understanding. "Maybe that's it. Well, I hope you enjoy," she says before walking away.

"Thanks," I mutter, letting out a deep breath.

I lift my hand, knocking softly on London's door. There's a feeling in the pit of my stomach that I can't quite explain. It's almost like a nagging, warm feeling that also twists my insides into knots.

She swings the door open quicker than I expect, almost like she was waiting just inside it for me to show up.

I won't lie, the thought of that makes me smile. Although, I'm not sure why. All these emotions I shouldn't be having are confusing the hell out of me. She shouldn't be making me feel this way, and I shouldn't be letting her. Yet somehow I can't seem to control the way I feel around her.

"Hey," she says shyly, a blush creeping to her cheeks.

"Hi," I respond, shifting from one foot to the other. She stays in the doorway, studying me. "You gonna let me in or make me stand on the porch all night?" I ask sarcastically.

"Right, come in." She motions for me to step through the door.

When I'm inside, we head to the kitchen. London stands awkwardly next to the counter, chewing on the corner of her lips. And I realize that we've rarely been alone and not ended up in a heated make out session. Shit, what the hell's wrong with me?

"So," I say.

"So," she repeats.

I don't know what the fuck to do. I really want to pull her into my arms and kiss the hell out of her, but I'm sensing that's not exactly what she has planned.

I step closer to her, putting my hands on her waist. "What's the plan for tonight?"

She turns her head to the side, hiding her eyes and mumbling, "I thought we could do dinner and maybe watch a movie. And in the process, get to know each other better."

Why does she look so uncomfortable? And scared? Is she worried I'll tell her that getting to know each other is not what this thing is about?

Technically, it isn't, and I really shouldn't agree, but the skittish look on her face pulls at my heartstrings. I should keep this about just sex, but how do I say no to a woman who looks as beautiful and worried as she does?

I don't. That's how. But I will remind her the reason we're doing this in the first place.

"Sounds good, but I think you're forgetting one very important detail." I nudge her arm, pinching her side affectionately at the same time and forcing her to glance my way.

"What's that?" she asks, batting her lashes and playing innocent.

There she is.

"This," I growl, pulling her forcefully to me and meeting her lips in a brief but passionate kiss.

She leans back. "Oh, right, well I thought that was a given." She winks and then smirks, instantly turning me on.

"Of course it is." I look at the counter, noting a couple of take-out bags. "What's in those?" I point my head towards the bags.

She steps out of my embrace, her warmth leaving me instantly, and walks around the counter to open them. "I thought I'd introduce you to the best burgers in the world," she says, pulling some takeout boxes from the bags.

"The best burgers in the world?" I question, wondering if she's ever traveled the world.

"Well, maybe not the best burgers in the world, but the best in South Carolina."

"And you've tried every burger place in the state?"

She quirks her head to the side, pouting her lips. "Don't be a smartass. You know I haven't, but that doesn't mean they aren't the best."

She opens the lids of the boxes, and the smell of the greasy beef makes my stomach growl.

"They sure smell like the best," I say, chuckling.

She places the burgers on some plates and adds fries, which also look amazing. "I told you," she mutters, carrying the plates over to the table where condiments, napkins, and silverware are already laid out.

We both take a seat. I feel London's eyes on me, staring like she's waiting for me to do something. "Why are you looking at me like that? You're making me nervous."

"Try it," she insists, pointing at the burger.

I crinkle my brows. "You want me to try it while you watch?"

"I want to see your reaction when you eat the best burger you've ever had."

"You're weird," I note, picking up the juicy burger.

"I know." She smiles, shrugging her shoulders.

I can't help but laugh. Seems to be all I do around her.

I bite into the burger, grease dripping off my fingers. I moan as the flavorful burger hits my taste buds. "Fuck, this is delicious!"

"Told you," she states, diving into her own burger.

I'm struck by the fact that she isn't afraid to eat what she loves in front of me. The women I date in Hollywood would never dream of eating a burger in front of me. I think that's what pulls me to her, the fact that she's so different from what I'm used to. She has such a confidence in who she is that she doesn't seem to care what anyone else thinks, and that's not something you see often in Hollywood or anywhere really.

Maybe that's why she makes me forget so easily, makes me feel things again.

"So, how's therapy going?" she asks around a bite of burger.

My ears perk up at the word, and I quickly chew the burger in my mouth. "It's going well," I say.

"That's good," she nods, her lips parted like she still has something to say. "You've been going for a couple weeks now, right?"

"Yea," I draw out slowly.

"Do you think it's helping?"

That's a good question. I haven't really thought about if it's helping or not, but now that she mentions it, I think it is. I don't feel as weighted down as I used to, and I'm finding it easier to joke and laugh again. I'm still haunted by the memories, and sometimes, the pain of what happened still becomes too strong, but I know with more sessions, I could be myself again.

Nineteen
London

Dinner was good, but not quite what I'd intended. We talked about all the basic stuff like the weather and the town, and how his therapy sessions were going. I still have no idea what causes him to just freeze in the middle of something and go into what almost seems like a tormented panic. I didn't really expect him to talk to me about it, but it would have been nice to know more about the man I had taken to my bed.

I suppose I should be grateful knowing that he's even attending the therapy sessions, and that they seem to be working. Even I've noticed a change in his personality. He seems lighter, especially when he's joking or teasing with me. His eyes don't hold the same dark expressions they did only weeks before. Don't get me wrong, I still see those dark emotions swirling in their depths, but there's a lot more light in them.

Now, some superhero movie that Jamie filmed a while ago plays while Jamie and I sit on either end of the couch, staring sightlessly at the screen. I'm pretty sure neither of us are paying attention to it, which doesn't matter since I've seen this movie a thousand times thanks to Brayden.

No, we're far more focused on the individual thoughts running through our minds. At least, I am.

All of this is so weird, this whole "fling" thing. I don't know how to do this stuff. I've only ever been in relationships where we go out on dates, and nothing happens until like date three. This is all foreign territory for me.

I twist my hands in my lap and my leg bounces up and down. I steal a look at Jamie. He's staring at the TV, but he frowns as if he's in deep thought.

"Are you even watching the movie?" I ask, still studying him from the side.

He shakes his head, not looking at me. "Nope, you?"

"Nope, I've seen it too many times before."

"I've honestly only watched it once, but then again, I spent months living inside it," he chuckles absentmindedly.

"So, I should just turn it off?"

He nods.

I click the power button on the remote and shift to face Jamie on the couch, pulling my legs into my chest. "Are you okay?" I ask, not sure what else to say.

He seems to do this a lot. One minute, he's fine and joking around, then the next minute he's in his thoughts.

"Yea, I'm fine."

"I know that's not true. You wanna talk about it?"

"No," he says.

His deep voice makes me shiver. I really don't know what to think of this man.

"Do you want to talk about something else?"

"Not really," he mumbles, less harsh this time.

Now what do I do?

I sit, staring at him and formulating my thoughts. He doesn't want to talk, but I do. I know virtually nothing about him, and I would like to know at least something about the man I'm sleeping with. Although with the way he's acting, I'm not sure if it's even worth it anymore.

Too bad I can't seem to get away from whatever it is pulling me to him.

"Wanna tell me something about yourself?" I ask, trying to find something he'll talk to me about.

He glances my way, his eyes sad and his lids heavy. "Like what?"

"Anything," I say, shrugging my shoulders. "Your family, friends, Hollywood, childhood, whatever you want."

He shifts on the couch a bit, facing me. "You're not going to let me get away without telling you something, are you?"

I shake my head firmly. "Nope," I state, popping the 'p' at the end.

He sighs, crossing his arms in front of him. "Women," he mutters under his breath.

I laugh, shaking my head. "Why is it that at dinner you were so animated and happy and flirty, but now you're all broody and tormented?"

"I told you I'm fucked up and I meant it."

"True, you did, but I'm still curious," I say, stretching out my legs so my feet land on top of his thighs.

He doesn't push me away like I expect. Instead, he places his hands on top of my shins. "There's just a lot I'm dealing with. It hits me sometimes. I can't control when or where, but usually, when I'm with you, I can forget about it and live in the moment. It's just not always possible."

"Yea, I get that. Life sucks sometimes, and we just have to find a way to live through it."

"I'm still working on that part, but the counselor really is helping. She's teaching me how to deal with the waves and ways to cope with them when they do overcome me."

"That's great, Jamie," I say, smiling warmly at him.

147

I know he means what he says. I can see it in his eyes. He's trying, but I also know from personal experience that it's not always easy to just move on from the hard stuff. Sometimes, it stays with you forever.

Hell, it took me years before I could move on from what Hamish did, and don't even get me started on the way my mom treated me growing up. I still feel the sting of her ignoring me all those years, but it was the most painful in high school. For the longest time, I thought there was something wrong with me and that's why she hardly spent any time with me. It took me awhile to realize it was my mom's issue, not mine.

"So, what about your family? Are they Hollywood super stars too?" I ask, changing the subject. I don't want to push him too hard, too fast. The last thing I want is for him to run from me, especially since I want to help him.

He shakes his head. "My mom was from Brooklyn, and my dad grew up on a ranch in Montana."

"Wow, how did they end up together?"

"They met at a wedding, weirdly enough," he says, chuckling. "I still don't know how two completely different people ended up together, but they worked."

"They say opposites attract," I muse.

"That they do." He grins at me, and I can't help the tingly feeling I have in my stomach.

"My parents weren't so lucky. They were too different."

"Where are they now?" he questions, rubbing my legs with his hand and making me almost forget what we're supposed to be doing. Almost.

I take a breath. "My mom died right after Brayden was born, and I never knew my dad. I don't even know his name or where he lives. My mom never talked to me about him. It's funny how life seems to repeat itself. Where are your parents?" I ask, steering the conversation away from me.

"They died when I was young. My grandma raised me, and when she died, I decided to go to Hollywood. I'd always had this crazy dream to be an actor. Thought, why not," he pauses like he's thinking about something. "What did you mean by life repeating itself?" he finally asks.

I know what he's doing here, tossing this conversation back on me so he doesn't have to talk. Maybe if I give him something personal, he'll do the same. It's not like Brayden's dad is a secret. There are no such things in this damn town.

"You've noticed that Brayden's dad isn't around?"

He nods.

"He left not too long after I told him I was pregnant. Said he wanted nothing to do with us. It hurt me, but Brayden's better off without the jackass." Anger pulses through my veins, and I'd like nothing more than to hunt Hamish down and give him a swift knee to the balls. But he's not worth it. Never has been.

However, he gave me Brayden, and I can't ever be mad at him

for that.

"Ah," Jamie whispers, warmth lighting his eyes. "I've never understood men like that. How do you walk away from your own flesh and blood?"

"I wish I knew the answer." I sigh. I've often thought about reaching out to Hamish and asking that same question, but for what? It wouldn't change the facts. It wouldn't make him want anything to do with our son.

"Do you ever hear from him? Does he send child support or anything?"

"Nope, I do it all by myself," I mutter bitterly.

He shifts my legs off him and moves closer to me, pulling me into the crook of his arm. "Well, from what I can tell, you've done a great job on your own."

"Thanks," I say, peering up at him. My hand is splayed across his chest, and I feel the gentle beat of his heart. "On a less serious note, how the hell did you end up in Sunrise?" I trace circles on his dark shirt, waiting for his answer.

His fingers dance up and down my arm, sending a shiver up my spine. "I came here once when I was younger. Spent my first paycheck traveling up the East Coast. Started in Florida and went to Maine. I remember loving it here. It reminded me of the small town I grew up in. So, I felt like it'd be a good place to get away, where no one knows me."

"Well, I'm glad you decided to come here," I tell him, smiling up at him.

"Me too," he whispers, kissing the top of my forehead.

We sit there in silence, my head on his chest and his arms wrapped around me. I listen to his soft breathing, closing my eyes and letting it relax me. I feel safe, protected with him, even though I know he's hiding something.

I know I shouldn't let myself get comfortable in his arms. Moments like this will ruin me. I'll forget what we are, what we're doing here. And yet, I can't seem to make myself let go or pull away.

Gently, his finger tips my chin up. "You're not like any other woman I've ever met, and I don't know what to do with that."

I open my mouth to respond with a snarky comment, but he captures my lips with his before I have the chance. His fingers caress my cheeks while his mouth devours mine.

My hands roam up and down his chest. Our lips move greedily together, fighting for more and more. I have no doubt where this is headed, and I can't wait.

I don't give him the chance to make the first move this time around. I decide to jump all in.

I shift my body so I'm on top of him, my lips never leaving his. I slip my hands under his shirt, pulling it up over his head.

He laughs huskily as he moves his hands to my waist. "Someone's excited tonight," he states, ripping my shirt and bra off in one swift move.

"Impressive moves," I smirk between frantic, needy kisses.

"You ain't seen nothin' yet," he whispers, sliding my leggings off just as fast.

He flips me underneath him, pulling his pants off before climbing on top of me. His lips trail kisses along my neck, hungrily. "Are you ready for this?" he asks, meeting my eyes. I see the fire, the hunger deep within his hooded eyes.

"Hell yea," I mumble just before he plunges me into the best high imaginable.

Twenty

Jamie

How has it been four weeks since I came to Sunrise? It doesn't even seem possible that I've been here that long. Even more impossible to believe is the amount of time I've spent with London over the last week. Even when my past bubbles up and I go silent, she just acts like everything is normal and I like that she doesn't let me wallow in the pain.

I open the door to the cafe that's quickly becoming my favorite breakfast spot and find London and Brayden sitting in the back. I had smiled so damn hard when she texted me this morning asking for me to join them for breakfast. I weave my way between the tables and people, waiting for someone to stop and ask me for my autograph, but it doesn't come.

I love the feeling of normalcy that brings me. I spent so much of the last few months bombarded by press, but here in Sunrise, no one seems to give a damn about who I am. It's refreshing, and sometimes a major hit to my ego.

As I stop just in front of their table, Brayden lays the tablet he's playing on down in front of him and pats the seat next to him. "I saved you a seat, Mr. Jamie."

"Thanks, bud," I say, pushing back all the memories that want to assault me when I look at him. I count to ten and keep myself in the moment, just like the therapist said to do. I'm going to enjoy this normal moment if I have anything to say about it.

"Hey, how are you today?" London greets, smiling brightly. I love her smile and how warm it makes me feel. She has a comforting smile, one that just makes you feel cared for even when she doesn't know you.

"I'm alright," I answer, playing with the rolled silverware in front of me. "Have you ordered yet?"

"No," Brayden says. "We were waiting for you. Mom says it's rude to order before everyone arrives."

I chuckle, ruffling his hair. "She's right, but I wouldn't have minded.

Brayden glares at his mom. "See, I told you. You made me starve for nothing."

London rolls her eyes and scoffs, "You're hardly starving, B."

"My stomach is literally eating itself," he insists.

I lean back in the chair, laughing. "Do you want me to go up and order?" I ask, needing to step away for a moment and collect myself.

London waves me off. "No need. The owner is my best friend. She, or the third member of our trio, always comes out to take our order. It's their excuse for coming out to talk, especially when they're busy."

As if on cue, a tall, dark-haired woman steps up to the table. She fist-bumps Brayden and gives London a hug. She stops when she realizes I'm sitting here as well. "And who might you be?" she asks, eying me up and down with a seductive smile.

London slaps her on the arm. "Sabrina," she hisses. "Stop being weird."

"I'm not being weird. I'm just checking out this extremely handsome friend you have here."

"Sabrina," London says firmly. "This is Jamie." She lifts her brow like she's hinting at something.

I can't help the curiosity that flows through me or the way it makes me feel, knowing there's a possibility she's been telling her friends about me.

Her lips form an "Oo." She reaches out a hand to me. "Sorry about that, I was just messing with her. I'm Sabrina. London's best friend. Nice to meet you."

I shake her hand in return. "Nice to meet you, too. This is a nice place you have here."

She laughs. "Thanks, but I don't own this place. The pregnant woman with the large teddy bear following behind her is the owner."

"Oh, and speak of the devil," London chimes, a bright smile on her face as a young woman steps up to the table. I recognize her immediately as the woman who served me the other day.

"Having another party without me?" she asks, stopping next to Sabrina.

"Not our fault you're too busy for us now that you have a man in your life full time again," Sabrina mutters out of the corner of her mouth.

"Where is Hunter?" London questions, searching the room for him. "It's odd for him to not be attached to your hip."

"I know, right? He's watching Hannah for the day, and I've never been so happy that his mom had things to do and couldn't watch her." The woman, whose name I still don't know, says in response to London's comment.

I look back and forth between the women as their friendly banter continues. I can barely keep up with them, they're talking so fast. I just sit back, letting them go until the woman looks at me.

"Wait a minute, I know you!" She eyes me intently, like she just realized I was sitting here.

I shift uncomfortably under her gaze. You'd think I'd be used to scrutiny since I'm literally under it all the time, but no, I still hate being the center of attention. I'm very aware of the irony of that with my job.

"Ki, this is my friend, Jamie," London introduces us, a far too sneaky smile on her face. Has she been telling this 'Ki' about me, too? I should be upset, but I'm fucking flattered instead.

Ki's eyes widen with recognition. "Of course, I thought I recognized you the other day. London told me you were in town."

London hisses Ki's name much like she did to Sabrina a few minutes ago. She glares at her like an angry cat waiting to pounce.

I smirk at Ki and egg her on, knowing it will annoy the shit out of London. "Oh, really?"

I'm very aware of London's glare now on me, but I don't look at her. I don't need to though; the burn from her gaze against my skin is enough to let me know she's looking my way and it wakes up a certain part of me that really shouldn't be awake right now.

"Moving on," London states. "We're here for food. Would you like to feed us?" Her tone is rather harsh and sassy, but the girls laugh it off like it's nothing.

"Of course we will," Ki responds, still laughing. "You tell Sabrina what you want and she'll get it made."

Sabrina's head snaps to Ki. "Um, excuse me. Why can't you do it?"

"Pregnant lady, remember? I have to take it easy," she mocks, pointing to her belly.

"Oh, whatever. You only pull that shit when it's convenient

for you," Sabrina muses, rolling her eyes.

"Isn't that how it's supposed to work?" Ki laughs, turning to leave. "Nice to meet you, Jamie. I hope to see you again soon."

I nod toward her as she walks away, stopping at a table a few feet over.

"So, what do y'all want?" Sabrina asks.

We place our orders, and she disappears to the back room.

"Well, that was fun," I chuckle, noting the wrinkles around London's eyes as she frowns. She still looks gorgeous even when she's upset.

"If that's what you want to call it," she mutters, a hint of amusement in her blue eyes telling me she found it fun as well.

"I like them. They seem nice. Down to Earth."

"I like them, too," Brayden pipes up, peering over the tablet in his hand.

"Yea, they're pretty cool. Annoying, but cool." She smiles. "They've been through a lot with me. Definitely a good group to have around."

"I can see that," I say. They may have teased each other or given each other crap, but what are friends for if they don't do that? I may not have a lot of friends, but I know what they should be like.

"So, what are your plans for today?" London asks, rolling a napkin up in her hands and then unrolling it again.

I shrug my shoulders. "Nothing, why?"

"We're going to play mini golf and go go-kart racing to

celebrate the end of my first week of school," Brayden tells me excitedly.

"That sounds fun." I stare at London, waiting for her to ask me to join because I know that's where this conversation is going.

A blush creeps to her cheek and she smirks. "You wanna join and get your ass kicked at mini golf?"

I beam, lifting my brows. "The better question is, are you ready to get your ass kicked on the go-kart track?"

London squints her eyes and places her hands on her hips. Her face is filled with exaggerated shock with a twinkle of amusement at the corner of her lips. "Are you seriously questioning my go-karting abilities right now?"

"What if I am?"

"You. Me. Race on the go-karts. Loser buys dinner," she says with so much confidence that I'm pretty certain I will be buying dinner tonight. I can't help the stupid grin that covers my face or the excitement I feel deep within.

I shouldn't agree to this. I'll be crossing yet another line that will move us past fling and to something more. But aren't we friends, too? So, is it really crossing a line? And do I even care about the fucking line anymore?

Not really. At this point, all I care about is forgetting every shitty moment of the past, and whenever I'm with London, I can.

"Deal," I agree.

She's sexy, sassy, and the kindest person I know.

A Famous Kind of Love

I could have any girl I want, but I want London.

Twenty-One

London

I'm genuinely offended that Jamie thinks I won't kick his ass at go-karts.

Like what, I'm a girl, so I can't possibly be better at this than him?

I should have confronted him about it, like the feminist I try to be, but I'd rather just show him by beating his ass on the track.

Which is exactly what I plan to do, even though I've already crushed him at mini golf. Okay, technically, Brayden crushed both of us, but I came in second and that's what really matters.

This feeling is kind of nice. I feel empowered. Competitive.

Strong. Sometimes, I forget I have it in me. I get so caught up in my crazy busy life that I forget to have fun. But, not so much since Jamie showed up.

I follow the go-kart track guide's directions to the locker room to put on my overalls, gloves and helmet. I really want to find some war paint and swipe it across my cheeks like the warrior I am.

But I don't for two reasons: One, it's slightly excessive, and, two, there's none in here. In fact, there isn't much in here at all, just some old beat-up lockers and dirty, worn uniforms and helmets.

The lockers look like they barely made it out of high school hell with all their graffiti and scratches, and don't even get me started on the track gear. It looks like it was worn in some kind of ferocious Viking war with all the slashes, holes, and stains.

It makes me wonder what goes on in here on a regular basis.

Once I'm dressed, I head out to the track where Jamie and Brayden wait.

"What took you so long? Did you get lost on your way out?" Jamie's smirk and sparkling eyes make him look ten times more gorgeous than usual. Way better than the dark, brooding side of him. Although, I like that side too.

I position my arms on my hips and cock my head to one side. "A girl's got to look good when she kicks some ass."

Jamie busts out laughing in his deep, baritone voice, giving me chills. The sound of his laughter does crazy things to my body, jumbling up my words and kicking my heart rate up unnaturally high.

Just then, a track employee steps up to us. "Hello, I'm Josh, and I'll be helping you on the track today. We're going to briefly go over the rules, how to drive, and some other important things before we begin."

He spouts off his rehearsed spiel, and Brayden bounces up and down with excitement like Tigger from Winnie-the-Pooh.

The track employee laughs. "How old are you?"

Brayden stops jumping and puts on a serious face. "I'm eight."

"You're still a little too young to ride on your own little man. So, you'll have to ride with your dad," the man explains, studying Jamie with a questioning look.

Jamie looks over his shoulder at me, a thousand different emotions swirling around his eyes, but his face remains still. He looks like he wants to protest, but he doesn't.

I see the wheels turning in his mind. He's not Brayden's father, but he also doesn't want to ruin this moment for my little boy and I'm grateful that he's letting my son have this moment without correcting it.

"Hey, aren't you that actor? The one in all the action movies? Jameson Decker?" the employee asks, a little light bulb finally going off in his head.

Jamie nods, looking unsure about what will happen next.

"Dude, I love all your movies. My dad and I watch your movies together all the time. Do you mind if I get an autograph?" He holds a scrap of paper and pen out to Jamie.

"Of course," Jamie takes it and smiles, signing the paper. When he hands it back, he says, "Could you not mention that I'm here? So far, no one else has realized who I am, and I'd like to keep it that way."

The young man nods vigorously. "Yes sir, your secret is safe with me."

A few minutes later, they give us the go ahead to climb in the go-karts. I know I missed all the rules they were going over back there, but I'm 99% sure I remember how to work one of these things.

I mean, I used to do it all the time. Surely, it's like riding a bike. Guess I'll find out in 3...2...1!

I hit the gas hard when the light turns green. The go-kart shoots out from underneath me, the engine's power forcing me back into the seat.

I come up to the first turn and spin the steering wheel to the right, releasing the pedal just enough to make it around the turn without flipping it.

Jamie and Brayden pass me on the inside of the turn, but I'm on his heels, pushing the gas to the floor and urging it to move faster.

I am not paying for dinner tonight. I repeat: I am not paying.

Mostly because I'm broke and can't afford to after our day here, but that's not the point.

I will win this race and rub it in Jamie's face. I'm not going down without a fierce fight because I am a *warrior*.

I slam the pedal as far down as it will go, and the go-kart leaps alive with extra power. I'm swerving around the turns like a pro and manage to slip around Jamie just as we round the last turn.

Just a little bit further.

I push the go-kart forward with positive energy and thoughts.

Come on. You can do it.

A few feet further.

Just a little more.

The boys fall further behind me as I cross the finish line. I scream for no real reason other than to let out all my adrenaline and excitement, since no one can actually hear me over the roar of the engines.

I bring the go-kart to a stop at the entrance to the track and climb out, tossing my helmet into it like a seasoned pro. The biggest grin is plastered all over my face as I wait for Jamie and Brayden. My heart pumps so fast and my blood races through my veins. Man, I love the feel of victory.

"No fair!" Brayden pouts, his arms crossed tight in front of him as he approaches me.

"What he said!" Jamie points his thumb at Brayden.

"You're just upset because you have to pay for dinner," I point out, lifting a brow at Jamie. Then, I turn to face B, crinkling my brows. "But why are you mad?"

"A girl beat me. Girls aren't supposed to beat boys."

"Why do you think that?"

He doesn't respond, choosing to shrug his shoulders and study the pavement under his feet instead. His aversion to looking at me worries me a bit.

"B, talk to me," I prod, but he continues to stare at the ground and run his foot back and forth along the black sea.

Silence fills the space between us for quite some time before my son finally speaks. "A boy at school told me I was a girl because a girl beat me at running in PE class."

That boy's words are everything that's wrong with society and goes against everything I've tried to teach my son over the years.

I take a deep breath and count to five, forcing the rage boiling up inside me back down into nothing. They're just kids.

I lean down to his level and put my hands on his shoulders so he's looking directly at me. "I want to make one thing clear - that boy was wrong. Sometimes girls are going to be better than you at some things, and that's okay."

"But I'm supposed to be stronger and faster than girls."

"No, you're not, B. Boys might be physically stronger than many girls, but not always. Some girls work really hard to beat the boys. She was probably faster than you because she runs often, and you hate running."

"I do hate running."

"You get that from me," I admit, laughing softly. "There's always going to be someone better than you. You can't be good at everything. It's just not possible."

"I guess that makes sense."

I smile and point my finger over my shoulder at Jamie. "Just ask him how he feels about losing to a girl today. I bet he'll say it wasn't that bad."

Jamie's feet squish against the pavement as he steps forward. He's so close I can feel the heat radiating off his body. It makes me all weak and tingly inside, and I definitely shouldn't be feeling this way in such a serious moment.

He clears his throat. "Your mom is right. I'm not mad about losing to a girl...I'm just mad I have to pay for dinner."

I turn a glare on Jamie, and he winks. My body melts to putty. Ugh, why can't my body just be normal around him?

Twenty-Two

Jamie

"So, you're not mad at Mom?" Brayden asks me, the familiar feeling of guilt evident across his face.

I step in front of London and look him straight in the eyes. "Not at all. She went out, raced, and won because she's good. There's no reason to be mad at her for that."

He chews on his lip, clearly thinking through what I've said. Finally, he nods his head slowly in understanding. "I'm sorry, Mom," he apologizes.

"It's okay," she assures him, standing and giving him a side hug.

"Now that we've got that resolved, what do y'all think about getting dinner?" I ask, noting the shock on London's face as she stares at me.

"Did you just say y'all?"

"Sure did."

"I think you've spent too much time in the South already," she states, and I laugh.

I disagree. I think I haven't spent near enough time here yet, and I'm not really sure what to do with that.

So, I simply turn the conversation back to food, and we make our decision to head to the diner.

Not even a half hour later, we're seated in a booth at the Sunrise Diner. I haven't been in here before, but it has a retro feel to it that I like. Worn, red leather covers the booths and chairs while bright red paint shines on the walls. It's almost like I stepped into a Coca Cola ad or something.

I pick up the plastic covered menu and read through the different meals even though I already know what I'm going to get - the best damn burger around. I've been dreaming about these burgers since that night at London's house.

"I think I'm going to have a salad with a side of fries," London announces, laying her menu on the table.

"Doesn't a side of fries defeat the purpose of ordering a salad?" I ask, eying her with a questioning gaze.

She shakes her head in defiance. "Absolutely not. They

balance each other out," she insists.

I swear, this woman. I can't explain it. She's unlike anyone, and I love it.

"I'm pretty sure that's not how it works," I say, quirking a brow at her.

"Works for me," she responds, shrugging her shoulders.

I just laugh, thinking about how much I like her logic. "I think I'm going to go all-in and do a burger and fries."

She smirks my way. "I told you they were the best."

"I won't lie, I've been dreaming about these things for the last week."

"I've been dreaming about chicken nuggets," Brayden states, placing the kid's menu down on the table like his mom.

"You are a chicken nugget, B. I swear that's all you eat." London laughs, squeezing him into her side.

He crosses his arm and squints his eyes. "It's not all I eat. I eat pizza, too." He says it in such a serious tone it makes me laugh.

"Fine, pizza and chicken nuggets," London chuckles, ruffling his hair.

His face is still hard and serious, and I can't tell if it's for show or if it's genuine. But I know it's a big deal for him.

An older woman with a name tag that reads Mary steps up to our table. Her red and white uniform blends in nicely with the surroundings, but her dark hair with gray streaks stands out in contrast. She looks as though she's a fixture in this diner with a warm smile on her face that tells me she loves her job and the people.

"Evening, London, it's been a little while since you've been in to eat," she greets.

"Sorry, Mary, I've been on a takeout kick lately. I just can't seem to make myself eat out after a long day when I could curl up on my couch and eat instead."

Mary laughs a hearty laugh and puts a hand on London's shoulder. "Trust me, honey. I get it."

The older woman turns to me. "And who might you be?"

I tip my hat to her. "Jamie, ma'am. Nice to meet you."

"The pleasure is all mine," she says, fanning herself exaggeratedly.

The funniest thing is I only ever get that reaction from the older women. The younger ones bat their eyelashes and put their hands on me subtly to show their attraction. I think I prefer the blatant actions over the shy and sly ones.

Mary laughs and shakes her head. "Okay, what can I get y'all to eat tonight?"

We place our orders, and she takes off back to the kitchen.

"I like her," I state.

"Of course, you do," London teases. "She was fawning over you. She's clearly good for your ego."

"What does fawning over someone mean?" Brayden asks, looking up at his mom.

"It means that you pay a lot of attention to someone or flatter them by saying lots of nice things," London explains.

Brayden nods his head like he understands, but his face is still crinkled with confusion. "Okay," he says. "So, if you like someone, you fawn over them?"

London tilts her head. "Yea, I guess so."

"Okay," he says again.

Silence falls around the table. Brayden looks as though he's still trying to understand, and London looks deep in thought, staring down at her twisted fingers.

"Does that happen to you a lot?" London asks, breaking the silence.

"What?"

"Women paying extra attention to you." Her voice is shy and her cheeks blush.

"Usually, yes. It's a lot worse when they realize I'm a movie star. It's not been too bad here though."

"Has anyone recognized you since you've arrived?"

I shrug my shoulders. "If they have, they haven't said anything to me about it, which is a good thing."

"They probably haven't put two and two together. We're a pretty small town that doesn't pay much attention to the outside world." She smiles at me.

"I've noticed, and I'm not complaining. It's exactly what I needed." I smile back.

"I pay attention," Brayden says, joining the conversation. "I knew you were my favorite movie star as soon as I met you."

I glance at Brayden. "I know you did, bud. How did it feel meeting your favorite movie star?"

"It was really cool but spending today with you was even better. It didn't even feel like you were a movie star. It felt like you were my friend," he states simply.

"That's because you are my friend," I respond, a tear prickling the corner of my eye. I force it away along with the pain. I'm not going to ruin this moment with tears.

"You're my friend too, Mr. Jamie," he says, and I'm not sure I can hold all the emotions back much longer. All the guilt, sadness, disappointment, regret, happiness, and hope feel like too much, but I do my best to put them back inside their little bottle in my heart.

I can let them out later when I'm alone and have time to process each of them.

"So, Brayden, what's your favorite movie I made?" I ask, trying to avoid the whirlwind I'm feeling inside.

He taps his forefinger to his chin. "Hm, I don't have a favorite movie. I like them all, but I like you better when you play a superhero," he explains matter-of-factly.

I chuckle. "Why do you like the superhero me better?"

"Because you help people. Mama says that's the best thing we can do in life." He shrugs his shoulders and reaches to pull his tablet out of his backpack.

His words ring clear as day in my ears. If only he knew the

truth, that sometimes I hurt people too. I don't want to be that person though. I want to be the one that helps people again, that has life and happiness inside him.

This family is slowly changing me, bringing me back to life. I can feel it with every part of me. I swore I'd never allow myself to love after everything that happened, but what if the universe doesn't give me that choice?

What will I do then?

Twenty-Three
London

I won't lie, I thought that moment at dinner the other night between Brayden and Jamie was beautiful. If I was seeing things correctly, I'd swear there was a tear in Jamie's eyes, but I'm probably just seeing what I want to see. It doesn't matter though. That day was damn near perfect.

My cell phone buzzes loudly on top of my metal office desk which has seen its better days. The sound echoes through the small space. I pick it up and click the answer button without checking to see who it is. "Hello," I say in my formal phone voice, forgetting I'm answering my cell phone for a minute.

"Why do you sound so professional on the phone?" Ki asks disgustedly on the other end.

"What the hell do you mean? I sound like I always sound," I respond.

"No, you don't. It's like you have a special voice reserved only for phone calls, and it's so professional."

"So, now, you're saying I'm not usually professional. Gee, thanks," I say, mocking her with sarcasm.

"You know that's not what I meant," Ki *tsks*, and I laugh.

"I know."

I hear a loud buzzing sound in the background and Ki screaming something I can't make out over the noise at the top of her lungs. The sound stops just as fast as it started.

"Sorry about that. Sabrina decided that it was a good time to mix up some dough, even though she clearly saw I was on the phone." The last part sounds muffled as though she's directing it away from the phone.

I hear Sabrina argue in the background, but she's not loud enough for me to make out exactly what she's saying.

"Sometimes, you two are too much for me," I note, chuckling at their banter.

"Okay, I think we're good now," she pauses. "Hunter and I want to do a little barbecue sometime soon, and I wanted to check on your schedule first before we made any decisions."

"Aw, that's so thoughtful," I say, mocking her once again.

"Yea, yea, yea, when's your next weekend off?"

I look up at the ceiling, mentally calculating when my next day off is. Shit, I can't remember. I pull the schedule up on my laptop, searching through it. I'm not sure why I didn't do this in the first place.

"Um, looks like I work this weekend, but I have next weekend off," I say, drumming my fingers on the desk.

"Perfect, that should work great. That's the first week of fall I think, so it could be like a fall bash."

"Oh shit, it's fall already?"

"Mhm, usually happens after school starts. But I'm sure with all that amazing celebrity sex you're having you've lost track of time," Ki coos over the line.

"How do you know I'm having sex with him?" I ask, my cheeks heating up like an ant under a magnifying glass on a hot day.

"Because you'd be stupid not to. Besides, your question just confirmed it for me." I can hear the amusement in her voice.

"Whatever. I better get back to work. I'll see you soon."

"Don't forget about the barbecue," she states in her mom voice.

"Right. Not this weekend, but next weekend. Got it. I'll be there," I say, hanging up after our brief goodbyes. I lay my phone on the desk beside me and sigh.

"Where will you be the weekend after next?" A deep voice makes me jump and sends my heart racing a thousand miles a minute.

I cover my heart with my hand. "Geez, Lousie, you scared the living day lights out of me."

Jamie chuckles, leaning against the doorway to my office and looking so damn sexy I could eat him up. I shift uncomfortably in my chair. "How'd you get back here?"

"The girl at the front desk told me I could come back when I told her I brought you lunch," he says, lifting a takeout bag up for me to see.

"Remind me to have a chat with her about letting strangers back here," I say, brushing nonexistent particles off my shirt.

He steps inside my office and practically fills the room, his broad shoulders making it feel even smaller than usual in here. "I'd hardly say we're strangers." His voice is seductive and deep, and his smirk tells me exactly what he's thinking about.

I cross my legs, trying to keep the tingling feeling between them from growing too strong. "Yea, probably not so much anymore, but ya know, it's the principle of it. Technically, no guests are allowed back here."

"Even the ones you're sleeping with?" he asks, winking in a suggestive manner.

"Especially those ones," I say, lifting a brow and daring him to argue with me.

"Why's that?"

"Because they think office sex is fun, and they might get me in trouble," I challenge, with a devious sneer.

He laughs. "Oh, I could definitely get you in trouble, but I'll try not to."

I nod. "That would be greatly appreciated."

He walks to the desk and sets the food on it, taking a seat in the one and only chair I have in my office. "You never did answer me. What plans do you have next weekend?"

"Just a barbecue with Ki," I explain, smiling.

"Am I invited?" he asks, eying me curiously.

"If you want to be, sure, but I assumed that might be too much for you. I mean that would be like we're announcing we're ... doing something together or whatever." My words come out all flustered, and I don't know why saying this makes me so nervous.

"Well, I mean, we are doing something," he chuckles.

"Yea, each other," I blurt, immediately regretting it as my cheeks flame red.

His intense stare burns a hole in my skin. I need to do something to put out the heat burning between us right now.

I rub my hands together and paste on an excited smile, pulling the takeout bag to me. The Sunrise Diner's bright red logo stands out against the white plastic bag. "What did you bring me for lunch?" I ask, giddy and suddenly very hungry, my stomach growling to prove the point.

"Look and see." He points to the food.

I pull the boxes out and set them on my desk in a row. I open the first box, which is a salad, and I laugh. I can't believe he's paying that much attention. I think I can already guess what's in the second one. I open it and smile, glancing up at Jamie. "I thought fries defeated the purpose of a salad?"

"They do, but you like it that way so that's what I got."

"What did you get to eat?" I ask, nodding at the third box.

"Do you really have to ask me?"

I shake my head. "Stupid question. It's a burger, isn't it?"

"Of course," he says, reaching for the box and setting it in front of him on the other side of the desk.

"This wasn't necessary but thank you."

"You're welcome." His eyes twinkle with a smile that he tries to hide.

If he keeps this up, I'm going to forget all about how this is a 'just sex thing'. Each time he does something thoughtful for me, it makes my heart all warm and fuzzy. I know that's a bad sign and I should stop all of it, but I don't want to.

I'm enjoying all of it way too much that I'd rather risk the heartbreak than give him up. I know I'll regret that later, but I can't seem to care about that now.

A soft vibration sounds against the metal chair Jamie's sitting in just as I take my first bite of salad. He slips his phone from his pocket, clicks a button on the side, and slides it back in.

"Who was that?" I ask, wiping a drip of ranch from my chin with a napkin.

"Just my manager," he says, brushing it off with a wave of his hand and opening the box that houses his burger and fries.

"Do you know why he's calling?" I push, trying to get some kind of serious conversation out of him.

He shakes his head. "Not a clue. Probably wants to discuss how therapy is going and when I think I'll be ready to make my next movie."

His voice is nonchalant, care-free like the thought of leaving and making another movie doesn't bother him. I wish I felt the same way. Instead, my body is literally shaking. I always knew him leaving was a possibility, but I've allowed myself to live in this blissfully ignorant state for the last few weeks.

"Next movie?" I question, trying to sound calm even though I can feel my pulse in my throat.

"If I even decide to make another one," he says, shrugging his shoulders and taking a large bite of his burger.

"Do you think you will?"

He glances my direction, slowly chewing his burger and studying my face. "Honestly, I'm not sure."

My pulse evens out. Maybe there's still hope for us yet.

Twenty-Four

Jamie

Shit. Why did I invite myself to some barbecue with London and her friends? That's moving far beyond "just sex" and into "we're more" territory, but I couldn't help myself. There's something about her that makes me do crazy things like inviting myself to places I have no business going or bringing up making another movie.

I shake my head. We've already moved past the defined status and on to something else. A something I don't know how to fucking define and have no desire to. As long as I keep pretending this is still "just sex," everything will be fine.

At least that's what I tell myself as I stand on her doorstep, knocking and holding two pizza boxes in my hands.

The door swings open and Brayden's boyish grin greets me, punching me in the gut and reminding me it's not just London I have to worry about. Regret fills my heart, and I fight the urge to just hand over the pizzas and leave, even knowing doing that won't change a fucking thing. I'm already too close to this family.

Just the thought of leaving to make another movie makes me feel hollow and empty inside, and the look of pure fear in London's eyes yesterday at lunch didn't help with that feeling.

"Mr. Jamie, what are you doing here?" he asks excitedly.

Damn, what am I doing here? This is so fucking stupid and against all the rules I laid out for myself after the accident.

"I thought I'd bring some dinner over for you and your mom," I say, feeling my heart rate pick up as I continue to rethink this whole thing.

"Are you going to eat with us?" His grin widens.

"Brayden, who is…Oh, hey, Jamie," London says, the biggest smile on her face as she approaches the door. It hits me in the gut just like Brayden's did and yet makes me want to shove her up against the wall and kiss her with every part of my being.

I thought I was fucked up before, but I'm pretty sure it's even worse now.

All of this has become so much more complicated. I don't just want London for the sex anymore. I want to confess all my worries and guilt, ask her to be a part of my life for real, and figure out what the hell my future holds because right now I'm pretty sure I don't want to go back to my old life.

"Hey, just wanted to bring some dinner over," I tell her.

She motions for me to come in, and I'm so grateful to be inside the nice, air-conditioned room. One thing they don't tell you about the south is how hot and humid it is in the beating sun, even in the fall.

"Thank you. I was just about to make dinner, so perfect timing." She takes the pizza boxes from me and follows Brayden into the kitchen, laying the boxes in the center of the table.

"B, can you get the paper plates and napkins for me?" She asks, taking a seat at the table as Brayden rushes from the room to the pantry.

She turns to look at me with a curious gaze, and I walk over to the table. "You don't have to keep surprising me with food."

"I know, but I like doing it," I say before thinking through exactly what that statement means.

She smiles. "Well, I'll never turn down free food, but I don't want you to feel like it's something you need to do since we're…ya know." Her hand moves between the two of us like she isn't sure what to call us.

I can't blame her. I'm not even sure what we are anymore. I know this isn't what it started out as, and I know we need to talk about it, but I'm not sure what to say. I have a lot of decisions to make that I've been putting off for far too long.

"Yea, I know," I state. "I don't feel like I have to do anything. I just like spending time with you." I wink, taking the seat next to her and placing my hand on her thigh.

"You mean you like having sex with me." She smirks.

"That too," I whisper in her ear, pulling back quickly when Brayden's face flashes in my peripheral vision.

"Sorry I took so long. I had to pee on the way," Brayden apologizes with a mischievous smile.

London laughs softly. "Of course you did." She takes the plates from his hand and lays one out for each of us. "Okay, guys. Let's dig in."

She pops open the box and her mouth curves into a smile. "Meat lovers pizza, my favorite."

"Mine too," I say, picking up a piece and putting it on my plate.

This woman is literally the perfect woman, and for two people from different worlds, we seem to have many things in common. Both our parents aren't around anymore, either by death or choice. We both like the same greasy foods. And, we even have similar tastes in movies, which doesn't happen often considering I love action-packed ones.

She quirks her head to the side, studying me. "Yea, I can definitely see that."

"Why?" I chuckle, crinkling my brows and interested to hear her response.

She shrugs her shoulders. "I don't know. Meat lover's pizza just seems like a very manly pizza."

"But you like it, and you're definitely not a man," I acknowledge.

Her cheeks redden and she laughs. "Yea, that was a dumb sexist thing to say. Anyone can like meat lover's pizza."

I point at Brayden. "What about you? Is meat lovers your favorite pizza, too?"

He shakes his head. "I'll eat it, but I like plain old cheese pizza the best," he says, opening the second box. His face lights up when he sees the cheese pizza inside. "Yes!" he exclaims, fist bumping the air.

I chuckle, taking a bite of pizza. "I figured plain old cheese pizza was a good bet for a kid."

"Good thinking," London notes, moaning as she takes a bite of her pizza.

Oh shit, that sound makes me hard and wanting for more. I situate myself in my chair, ignoring the need pulsing through my veins. It's something that never seems to go away, even when I'm nowhere near her. It's an odd feeling for me.

"So, Mr. Jamie, when are you going to make another movie?" Brayden asks in between bites. I swear this kid always seems to know when to call an adult out. It's like he knew his mom and I just had this conversation yesterday.

"Not sure, bud. I'm taking a break from making movies right now."

"How come?"

London wipes her mouth with her napkin. "B, it's not our business why. We need to respect Jamie's privacy."

He nods, glancing my way. "Sorry, I didn't mean to be in your privacy."

I grin at his misuse of the word. "It's okay. There are a lot of reasons why, but mostly I just needed a vacation."

He thinks about that for a moment. "Yea, I need a vacation too, but we can't ever take one because of money."

That hits me square in the chest. I forget that there are people out there who can't do the things I do on a regular basis. I have so much that I take for granted, and I hate that.

It affects me even more when it's the woman and her son that I'm growing closer to every day. They're such good, kind-hearted people. They deserve to be able to do the things they want, and yet, money stops them.

I've been fortunate, I know that, and I've been smart about my money. I've even supported local charities and hosted fund-raisers, but right now, none of that seems important. It makes me wonder how many more families like this one are out there. How many people have to sacrifice the things they want to provide for the people they love?

"Brayden," London hisses angrily.

He shrugs his shoulders, frowning. "What? It's true. We never get to do anything because of money," he states so simply like it's just another normal fact about life. Except it shouldn't be a fact for anyone.

London's face sours. "We get to do a lot, B. Just not everything we want to. That's just how life works."

"I know, Mom," he sighs, finishing the last of his pizza. "May I go play video games?"

She nods, her frown wrinkling her face. "Sure."

He cleans up his stuff and leaves the kitchen.

"I'm sorry about that," London apologizes, playing with the half a slice of pizza still on her plate.

"Why? There's no need to be sorry."

She stares down at her plate, ashamed of what Brayden said, and that strikes me in the gut. I know I have far more money than them, but I never want her to feel embarrassed for all the hard work she does. Shit, I could buy this town with the money I have saved in the bank, but you'd never know it from looking at me.

"Yes, there is," she states firmly, and I'm thoroughly confused.

I lift my eyebrows and my face falls. "Why?" I ask again.

"Because it's far too serious of a discussion for whatever this is." She waves her hand between us, a gesture that's becoming familiar whenever she talks about our arrangement.

A sting of something I can't quite place my finger on surges through my heart. I want to say I'm hurt or sad, but I shouldn't be. She's not wrong, and yet, that doesn't stop me from feeling any of

188

these things.

"What if I want to know the serious stuff?"

She studies my face. Her eyes full of a hope that leaves me feeling empty and drained. It's a hope that believes I want more than sex.

We've blurred the line so much lately with this whole hanging out as friends on top of sleeping together that I don't know which way is up or down anymore.

Twenty-Five
London

"What if I want to know the serious stuff?" His words bounce around my head, but how can they possibly be true? How can he want to know the serious stuff?

I'm so confused. It's just sex. We're just friends. It's both. What the hell are we?

We've been spending so much more time together this last week. That first kiss over a month ago feels so far away now.

The worst part is now Brayden's heart is involved. Jamie

always wants to include him, which I love, but I also hate it. If this is only sex and he means what he says - that he can't give me more - then how will that affect Brayden?

Every single bit of this is becoming so much more complicated. Yet, I still find myself wanting to be with him every chance I get. Logically, I know it's stupid, but it doesn't seem to matter to my overly excited heart.

I also can't move past the possibilities. What if he can give me more than a sexual relationship? What if talking about the serious stuff proves that? But what if, in the end, it doesn't matter? What if he decides to go back to Hollywood and make movies again? I can't just pick up my life and go with him, not with Brayden to think about.

"London?" he questions, breaking into my thoughts.

"What if I don't think you really do?" I counter because sometimes honesty is the best policy.

He places his hand on my arm, squeezing tight. "I thought you wanted to talk, to get to know each other better. That includes the serious stuff, right?"

"Does it though? Because you don't ever want to talk to me about your serious stuff." Which drives me absolutely insane. Why should I be the only one to have the hard conversations and open up?

He turns away from me, hiding the sudden dimming of light in his eyes. "That's different," he says hard.

"How?"

"Because it just is." His voice is even more firm this time, telling me to back off without actually telling me, but I don't want to. Whatever it is we're doing has become something more. We've moved from barely knowing each other to spending practically every day together.

"It's not different. You just don't want to talk about it. And, frankly, I don't want to talk about my own sensitive subjects with someone who doesn't want to open up in return." I stand from the table, pushing the chair back so hard it nearly falls over.

"I told you I can't give that to you," he growls, staring out the bay window on the other side of the table.

"No. You said you can only give me sex. Yet, you're the one that keeps showing up at my office, the cafe, here. Do you even realize that you've spent every day with me for the last two weeks?"

He doesn't respond. He just continues to stare out the window, looking at what, I don't know. All I can see are palm trees and grass. There isn't even a damn bird in the trees.

I scoot the chair up to the table and remain silent. Mostly because I'm not sure what else I could say. Besides, I don't think anything I say would matter at this point.

He doesn't want to talk, and I'm not going to make him. I'm just not that type of person, but I'm also not the type of person to not call people out on their shit.

My hands rest on the back of the chair. The wood feels cool under my hands. Jamie doesn't take his eyes off the window, and I don't take my eyes off him.

I don't know why I'm doing this to myself. I'm falling for him more each day, and I just keep letting myself. At this point, I'm not sure I could stop if I wanted to. I just wish he'd give me something, just a little piece of hope that lets me know he feels something too, even if it's only friendly. At least that would let me know I'm not completely alone in my thoughts.

"I want to tell you," he finally speaks.

My heart races so fast I can almost feel it in my throat. "Then, why don't you?" My voice is soft, concerned, soothing. He's finally talking, and I don't want to scare him away.

"Because it will be real. So much more real than before. Here, there are no reminders of it. I can let myself fall into being with you. But if I tell you, that all changes." He looks at me, wrinkles of sadness around his eyes.

"But you told the therapist, right?" I ask defensively. He can talk to some stranger about it, but not me.

"That's different," he whispers.

Gah, I want to smack him. He's so infuriating with this bullshit. I wish I knew why he's so insistent on keeping his past to himself. I'm a natural talker, I like to talk things out as it helps me process everything. I know Jamie isn't like that, but it's so damn frustrating for a person like me.

And I know I could find out the truth for myself. All I'd have to do is read the articles online, but I want to hear it from him, not the press.

"Clearly, you're determined to be a stubborn ass about this, but I can be just as damn stubborn. I stand behind my statement, but I'll give it a rest for now."

He chuckles. "I know I'm going to have to talk to you about it eventually, but right now, I'd much rather do this." He stands from his chair, his lips inches from my face.

He leans in slowly, meeting my lips softly at first and then harder.

"Hey Mom," Brayden's voice instantly destroys the mood and forces me back quickly.

"Yea B," I say, spinning around to face him. His face is scrunched together as he looks between Jamie and me.

"Are you two boyfriend and girlfriend?" he asks, pointing at us.

"No," we both say a little too loudly.

"Then, why were you kissing?" His nose crinkles in disgust.

"Oh, uh…" I pause, not knowing what to say. Jamie snickers behind me, and I lift my foot, kicking him in the shin softly.

"Ouch," he mutters in my ear.

"That's what you get," I spit from the corner of my mouth. Brayden is still standing there, staring at me, and I still have no freaking clue what to say to him.

Sometimes, parenting sucks.

I take a breath and step towards him. "B, Jamie and I are just friends."

"Friends don't kiss, Mom," the tone of his voice makes me sound stupid and makes him sound overprotective.

"Some friends do."

"Why?"

Jamie snickers again, and I turn to face him. "Can you leave, so I can talk to B alone?"

He frowns, and I don't think he likes the idea, but he agrees anyway. "Sure, call me later," he says.

"I will," I respond, smiling softly in his direction.

Saying goodbye, he disappears out the front door.

I focus on Brayden again. "Look, I know it's weird and hard to understand, but sometimes people who are friends like each other and they kiss."

"But you don't kiss Aunt Ki or Aunt Sabrina?"

He's not wrong, but he's making this so difficult. Why does he have to be so darn observant and smart? Why can't he just accept my vague explanations and leave it at that?

I sigh. "It's complicated, B. Jamie and I like each other like boyfriends and girlfriends do, but we're just friends."

"Why?"

I wish that word didn't exist because it's annoying as hell to have to answer. But, also, it's a good question. Why are we just friends when it's clear we like each other more than that? I wish I knew.

"Because Jamie doesn't live here, and he'll be leaving soon."

The way his face falls nearly crushes my heart. "Oh, right, I don't want him to leave."

I drop down to his level and cup his cheek in my hand. "I don't want him to leave either, but that's the way life works sometimes. He has a job and a life, and if you want him to keep making movies, he'll have to leave."

"I guess that makes sense. Do you think he'll come back?"

"I don't know, B."

I honestly don't know, and it makes me feel like something heavy is sitting on my chest, crushing me into a thousand pieces. I don't want him to leave. What the hell do I do with that?

Twenty-Six
Jamie

L: Sorry about earlier. I was struggling with how to explain what he saw, and you laughing was not helping.

Me: Sorry, I couldn't help it, but I understand how that conversation would be difficult.

L: Yea, well I thought maybe we could finish what we started.

Me: Okay. What do you have in mind?

L: Room service, your room.

Me: Hell yea!

L: I'll be there after I get off work tomorrow and drop B

off with Sabrina.

Me: Sounds fucking perfect.

I read through the messages London sent last night, feeling my excitement pulse through my body. The last thing I expected was for her to suggest finishing that kiss, but damn is it a nice surprise.

I hadn't gone over there with the intention to have sex. I'd honestly just wanted to see her but being around her just made me horny as shit. And that intense conversation brought up a lot of things I really didn't want to think about. I needed to kiss her. I needed to sink into her to forget.

Yet, I also know that's a discussion we need to have, but I don't want to ruin what's going on between us. She means so much more to me than I ever intended, and I don't know what to do with that.

Although maybe she means finish the conversation? She didn't exactly clarify what we're going to finish.

Before I can think any more about it, a soft knock sounds on the door and I click my phone off, laying it on the table. I walk over to the door and open it, her sexy smile greeting me. She's wearing a tight, short black dress that accentuates her curves and sends my mind into a thousand different thoughts about what I will do to her tonight.

I move out of the way, letting her come in. She's holding a bag of food from the hotel restaurant. "So, that's what you meant by room service?" I nod towards the bag.

"Of course." She smiles smugly. "I get a discount at the hotel restaurant. What else did you think?"

I shake my head, laughing. "Shit, I don't know. Guess I figured it was an innuendo for sex or some shit."

She cocks her head to the side. "Well, I mean, I figured that would be dessert."

She heads to the coffee table and sets the food down then tosses a bag to the floor.

I love this. I love the way we can shift easily from serious back to whatever this is. And I love that the fact I didn't tell her anything last night didn't affect this thing we're doing. Although, I know that probably has more to do with the rules I laid out when we started this.

She sits down on the couch, and I take the seat next to her, pulling out the food. "This smells delicious. What did you order?"

"Roast chicken, potatoes, green beans, and fried apples."

My mouth waters as I open the plastic container and hints of garlic and cinnamon assault my nose. London hands me a plastic fork, and we eat in silence for a while. It's a comfortable silence, another thing I love about spending time with her.

I take a bite of the juicy, perfectly seasoned chicken. "This is perfection."

"It is really good." She smiles, stuffing some beans into her mouth.

"How was your day?" I ask, surprising myself by how genuinely curious I am.

She stops chewing and turns to me like I've lost my mind. I can't blame her. I know this is far out of the realm of sex only. I'm inching into boyfriend territory, but I can't help it. And if I'm being honest, I kind of like it. I want to know how her day was, what she went through, and everything she's thinking.

"It was good. Had the usual paperwork and such. You?" She whispers, sounding shocked.

"Oh, you know, spent the day working hard."

"Really?"

"Yea, watched a lot of TV, went for a walk, and even took a nap."

She punches me lightly on the shoulder. "You're such a goof." She laughs.

"And you're beautiful."

Her cheeks blush instantly, and a shy smile brightens her face. "Now, I know you're just being silly."

I situate myself so I'm facing her and place my hand on her cheek, rubbing small circles with my thumb. "I mean it."

"I know, and that's the problem," she says sadly.

"How is that a problem?"

"I'm forgetting what we are. Every time you compliment me or do something nice for me, it makes me think this might be turning into something real. I keep reminding myself that it isn't. I have to tell myself that you don't mean it."

I sigh, dropping my hand from her cheek. I don't know what

to do or say. I know I'm confusing her as much as I'm confusing myself, but I don't want to stop. I like giving her compliments and flattering her. I like making her feel special because she is special. She's so fucking special to me, and she deserves to know it.

Fuck, I really need to figure shit out.

"I know I'm not making this easy for you, but I can't help it. I like being with you and that makes it hard to stay away," I admit, more to myself than her.

I can't give her all of me because I'm not sure all of me is alive to give anymore. It's not just the guilt or regret. It's the fact that a piece of me died that day.

"I like being with you, too," she states, a small smile forming on her face.

"Then, let's just enjoy our time together, whatever it's turning into. Maybe it's not just sex anymore, but even if it isn't, I'm not ready to be done with you yet."

She doesn't look convinced, but a spark of hope tinkles in her eye. I don't mean to get her hopes up, and I don't want to make her think I will fall in love with her because I won't. I made a promise to myself not to, but what if it's not something I have control over?

I wasn't lying though. I'm not ready to give her up.

My therapist would enjoy this inner battle I'm dealing with now. She'd say it's about damn time I feel something other than guilt and agony. We've been working on how to deal with my bouts of guilt and how to forgive myself for what happened. I'm still a work in progress, but I'm getting there.

I brought up London in our last session. I don't know why. I guess I just wanted to talk to someone who didn't know either of us. We dug deep into the promise I made to myself, talked about why I felt the need to make that promise, and discussed if it would actually change anything.

I know it won't change anything, but even if I am finding my way back to who I was before the accident, it still doesn't feel entirely right. I don't feel like I deserve to be happy. That doesn't seem to be stopping me though.

Actually, it seems to be making me want her even more.

Fuck, my head is a mess. I need to figure this shit out because I'm not sure I could live with myself if I hurt her or Brayden, too.

"I'm not ready to give up on you either," she whispers, and those words undo me.

I take the fork she's holding in her hand and toss it on the coffee table, pulling her into me.

My breathing is heavy, labored. I don't know why, but those words are exactly what I need to hear.

Maybe I needed someone else to believe in me too. Maybe that's all I've needed since the accident, to feel like I have something to live for, like my life isn't a waste. Somewhere deep inside, I truly believe I should have died in that accident because I have nothing to give.

But maybe I have more to give than I thought.

I lean into London, inching closer and closer. My lips capture hers with mine. I kiss her with everything I have, I may be messed up, but I do everything I can to show her how I feel, even if I'm not willing to admit it myself.

I reach my hand around the back of her neck, digging my fingers into her hair and pulling softly. I deepen the kiss and she opens up for me, our tongues swiping fiercely against each other.

My hands move to her dress, pulling on the bottom and slowly rolling it up her body. I toss it to the side and take her in. "Fuck, you're gorgeous. Every inch of you is delicious," I growl, slipping my hands around her back and popping her bra off.

She reaches for my shirt, and I push her hands away. "No, let me take you in for a moment." I need to study her, to memorize every curve of her body.

I lean over top of her, forcing her to fall back against the couch. I start between her legs, trailing kisses up her stomach and making her squirm.

My lips find her breast, and I tug her nipple into my mouth, sucking on it hard and loving the little gasp she makes when I do.

My lips move further up, landing on her neck just below her chin. "I'm about to give you the best fucking orgasm of your life," I whisper into her ear.

"Promises, promises," she breathes, just before I capture her lips in mine once again.

Twenty-Seven

London

I snuggle into the warmth of his arms wrapped around me. After he gave me the best orgasm of my life, he then pulled me to the bed and proceeded to give me five more. I've never came that many times at once in my life.

I shimmy my body around in his arms, trying to get comfortable as the sun peeks through the window.

"Fuck, woman, are you trying to get laid again this morning?" he grunts in his sleepy voice.

"I mean, I wouldn't be opposed to it," I say, shrugging my shoulders against him.

He chuckles, kissing my neck and pulling me in tighter. "Of course you wouldn't."

We lay there in silence, and I revel in the feel of this big, strong, broody man, cuddling me in his arms. I don't know how long this will last - his attention, that is - but I'm going to enjoy it.

I hope it lasts a lifetime. I realized that last night when he was sending me into another universe. I don't want any of this to end. I mean I think I've known that for a while, but I haven't really admitted it because it's insane.

He's only been here a couple months give or take a week or two, and I'm already attached. I keep trying to tell him, hinting at it, hoping he'll end it before I fall too deep, but he seems to be falling just as hard as me.

Even if he hasn't said it, I want to believe it because it's in his every action. Just the way he compliments me or brings me lunch every day tells me he has some kind of feelings for me. If it were just sex, he wouldn't be doing those things, right?

I twist in his arms, rolling around to face him. He pops one eye open and smiles. "What are you doing?"

"Just wanted to look at you," I say, sliding my finger across the skin of his chest. His hand finds my waist and I suck in a breath. I want to say something else, to ask a million questions, but I don't know where to begin.

He traces circles on my hip, causing goosebumps to appear on my skin. His touch feels incredible, and it makes me want to fall even deeper into him.

I study his face, his eyes focused on his hands. He looks like he's somewhere far away, a dark, torturous place. He continues to trace circles on my hip as he speaks, "It was an accident."

I squint my eyes. "Accident?" I ask, having a feeling that he's still not really here with me or even speaking to me for that matter.

His eyes meet mine. "Yea, an accident. I didn't mean for it to happen."

"For what to happen?"

A million scenarios bounce around in my head, making my heart beat fast with fear. Was it the accident I saw in the headlines? Did he hurt someone? Did he have some kind of psychotic break? Was it someone he knew or a stranger?

I want to voice my questions, but I wait rather impatiently for him to continue.

He looks away again, a pained expression on his face. "It was so dark and rainy. I didn't see it until the last minute."

I want to ask what he didn't see. Instead, I breathe deeply, trying to calm my nerves. I'm afraid my thousands of questions will only stop him from telling me, so I wait again.

He chokes out a tortured laugh. "It was a fucking rabbit, but it startled me, and I swerved trying to miss it. A damn bunny. Who gives a fuck about a bunny?"

He pauses, swallowing hard and lifting his hand to his hair. My skin feels cold without his hand there. I place my hand on his chest, needing to feel him, to have that connection.

He looks down at my hand and covers it with his. "I never saw the car coming, not until it was too late. I couldn't go anywhere. I couldn't stop. The only thing I could do was slam on my breaks and let the collision happen."

I turn my hand and hook my fingers between his, squeezing and encouraging him to continue.

"Everything went black, and next thing I knew I was on my way to the hospital where they ran scan after scan and covered me in stitches. The cop came in to talk to me, told me they had to do an investigation," he stops, tears glistening in his eyes.

He sucks in a breath and starts again. "He told me an eight-year-old girl died in the crash. She was on the side of the car that had the most impact. She died almost instantly. My reaction took a child's life."

I watch the silent tears slide down his cheeks, and I find myself sniffling as well.

"They told me it wasn't my fault. I wasn't speeding, but I was on the wrong side of the road. The family is still fighting with my lawyers on a settlement. Shit, I'd give them everything I have if money would make it better, but I know it won't.

"Nothing will bring that little girl back. Nothing will make the pain go away, but God, I wish it would." He wraps his arms around me and pulls me into his chest.

My heart pounds in my chest. A little girl? The rational part of me knows it wasn't his fault. He didn't go out that night intending to hurt anyone. It was an accident.

But the mother in me wants to scream and yell. That could have been my child - my son in that car. God, he's the same age as that girl. How does a family come back from that?

His eyes bore into me, anguish spilling from their dark depths. I know he didn't mean it, and I know he feels the accident deeply. I saw him in that hotel room right after he arrived. He was a mess.

But he reached out. He started therapy. He became a part of my family whether I wanted him to or not. And as much as the mother in me wants to hate him for what he did, the part of me that fell for him can't.

So, I let him hold me. I don't know how long we lie like this in silence, but it doesn't matter. I let the feel of his warm body soothe me, sending me into a more relaxed state and reminding me that I can't change how I feel about him or what he did.

I listen to his breathing. It's heavy at first, but the longer we lay here the slower and softer it becomes, like having me in his arms relaxes him.

"Then, I met you," he whispers. "Something about you made the guilt and the pain lighter."

"I'm sure the therapist had something to do with that as well," I joke.

"Of course, she did, but you did as well. For the first time in a while, I could breathe normally again. I could joke and laugh. I could

A Famous Kind of Love

forget, and that made me feel even more guilty. Why should I get to forget if they don't?

"But even that guilt has started to fade. It's like you're helping me live again. I swear something died in me that day, leaving me broken, but I don't feel as broken anymore," he says, sounding sad.

"I told you therapy would help. Besides, those are good things," I insist against his chest.

"Are they though?" he asks, posing a good question. I want to believe that they are, but I also know that if I were that girl's parents, I'd want him to live with the knowledge that he destroyed my life for as long as he lived.

All of this is difficult. I have feelings for this man. I know I do. I want to comfort him, but I also want to comfort that family.

"Our past mistakes don't define us. They teach us a lesson, but they don't tell us who we are. You shouldn't let the guilt and the pain break you down," I say, knowing it's what we both need to hear. I know the past is the past. I've lived by that rule my whole life, but the line feels blurred right now. I don't know if this is something that should stay in the past.

"Why not? It's what I deserve," the pain in his voice breaks my heart.

Is it what he deserves? I want to scream yes into the night sky. I want to agree with him, but then I stare deep into his brown eyes. The wave of emotions soaking me to the core. He's suffering just as much as that family is, I can feel it deep within. He never meant to hurt anyone, and I know it's killing him inside to know he did.

So as much as I want to say it's what he deserves, I know no one deserves to live life like that, not even him.

"No one deserves to have half a life because of an accident that could have happened to anyone. You're not broken, Jamie. You're not dead inside. You're just in pain. And that pain will fade the more you begin to live your life." I turn my head, kissing his chest.

"So, you don't think I'm a bad guy?" His voice is strained.

"I think you can be a brooding asshole sometimes, but I've never thought you're a bad guy. In fact, I think you're one of the best I know."

"Why?" he mumbles, his voice sounding far away. "How can you think that after what I just told you?"

"Because you're kind to my son and me. You clearly care deeply. And you feel every emotion to your core."

He squeezes me tighter against his chest, his chin laying on my head.

"I don't deserve you," he whispers into my hair.

"Of course you do, because you deserve to be happy," I whisper, closing my eyes and letting his warmth flow into me.

This man. This big bear of a man thinks he doesn't deserve me, but he is so wrong. We both deserve to be happy, and that's all that matters.

Twenty-Eight

Jamie

Remind me again why I invited myself to a barbecue with London and her friends? Oh, that's right. Because I'm a fucking moron.

I tug on the hem of my plain black shirt as we walk up the short pathway to a backyard. I think London said this is Ki and Hunter's house, who I haven't met yet. Apparently, they just bought it or something? Shit, I can't remember anything with the way my nerves are racing through my body and twisting my stomach into knots.

I don't know why I'm so damn nervous. It's not like I haven't met London's best friends before, but this feels more official. It's like we're saying we're a couple to the whole damn world and that terrifies the shit out of me because I have no idea what the future holds for me or my career.

I know we're more than "friendly" friends now. After all, I told her everything that happened to me, and she didn't run away. That in itself tells me exactly how she feels about me.

However, it doesn't change the intense racing of my pulse or sweating currently going on.

I should have listened to London when I'd said I'd like to go. She'd tried to tell me that this would be a statement, but I didn't think anything of it at the time. Now, though, as we near the fence to the backyard, I'm starting to think she was right.

We stop just short of the gate. Brayden opens it and flies through without a care in the world, disappearing behind the now closed gate, but my feet don't move. They feel like they're glued to the pavement, far too heavy to lift.

London touches my arm, her face frowning with concern. "Are you alright?"

"Fuck, no. I'm nervous as hell."

She chuckles, rubbing her hand up and down my arm, which isn't doing shit to calm my nerves. "There's nothing to be nervous about. They don't bite."

Yea, that doesn't help either.

"I know," I grumble.

She moves to stand in front of me, both her hands grabbing mine. "You've already met my friends, so I know that's not the problem. What's really bothering you?"

Awe, shit. I hate the way she can read me sometimes. It's like she's known me all my life, not a month or two.

The late September breeze brushes along my skin, catching me off guard and giving me goosebumps. The sun beats down on my back, warming me up in contrast to the breeze.

I can't believe it's already September. How have I been here that long already?

"I don't know why I'm so nervous," I finally say, sighing. "I guess it just makes all of this more real."

She looks me straight in the eyes, passion lighting her eyes. "It is real. I know it's hard for you to deal with after everything that happened, but…"

I stop her before she can finish. "I know I deserve to be happy, and I need to stop punishing myself for something I had no control over."

I still hear her words from the other night, ringing loud and clear in my mind.

"Exactly," she smiles wide.

But I'm not smiling. She doesn't understand that it isn't that easy. It's not like getting back on a bike when you fall off. I can't just start living again. That's not how this shit works.

I never wanted to be broken. I never wanted to be so caught up in my mistakes that I forgot how to feel. And I sure as hell never wanted to relive that day over and over. But that's what happens when you fuck up and I'm still learning how to deal with the consequences, even after weeks of therapy. Although, I'll admit, I'm much better than before.

"Look, I know this is hard for you, but that's why I'm here, remember? To make it easier?" Her smile is sweet and perfect, and somehow, it manages to ground me back to reality.

She's right. This is why I haven't been able to stay away from her. She makes it easier.

"Okay, let's do this," I say, nodding my head firmly. My actions might show I'm ready, but my insides are still twisting.

She drops one of her hands, tugging me with the other one towards the gate.

I'll be damned if I'm going to fuck this up now. She means way too much to me, which is exhilarating and terrifying at the same time.

London swings the gate open and pulls me through with her. The backyard is larger than I expected, with a pool, patio, and colorful flower garden. Brayden runs through the yard with a little red-headed girl and several adults sit around a table, drinking and laughing.

"Are we late?" I whisper to London.

"No, but we would have been if you'd kept the meltdown going any longer," she teases.

I drop her hand, wrapping my arm around her waist and

pinching her on the ass. "That's what you get for being mean."

She just laughs and shakes her head.

We walk over to the patio, several people turning to look at us in the process. I recognize Sabrina and Ki, but I have no idea who anyone else is here. Ki stands next to a taller, red-haired man, his arm tight around her. I assume this is her partner, Hunter. An older couple sits next to them, laughing and telling stories.

What am I doing here?

I feel so out of place. This isn't my world at all. Small, intimate gatherings are foreign to me.

London guides me closer to the small group of people, introducing me as we go. "You remember Ki?" I nod. "This is her boyfriend, Hunter, and these are his parents, Rose and John."

She points to an older man with a gruff appearance. "And this is Ki's dad, Bennett."

She turns to Sabrina next. "And you know Sabrina."

"Hello. It's nice to meet you," I greet them, feeling slightly naked without my cap and shades to shield me from them.

"Glad you could join us." Ki smiles softly.

"Come on, let's get a drink," London says, dragging me toward a cooler and table.

I take a minute to breathe, away from all these strangers. For a celebrity, I should be much better in situations like this, but you never know how people will act around you. For example, I was in a bar for a friend's birthday and was mauled by a group of women, one of whom I had to get a restraining order against because she kept finding her way onto my movie set. Or one time, a man jumped me when I was coming out of a restaurant because his wife said she was having an affair with me.

I grab a beer from the cooler, snap it open, and chug a sip, letting the refreshing ale soothe me and wash away the memories of crazy fans.

"That wasn't so bad, was it?" London asks, sipping on some kind of lite beer I don't recognize.

"Not if you're used to this kind of thing," I say, drinking my beer a little faster than I probably should.

"What kind of thing? Barbecues?" Humor dances in her eyes, and I know she thinks I'm being stupid and messing with her. But I'm not.

"Yes, barbecues. And any other small gathering where people get to see the real me."

"Don't you do these kinds of things in Hollywood?" she asks, her eyes bright with curiosity.

"Of course, but they usually have so many people at them that I can hide in a corner, drink, and never actually have to talk to anyone. This is so much more personal. It's not something I'm used to."

"You mean that Jameson Decker, big bad movie star, is afraid of a small gathering?"

"I'm not afraid," I scoff, knowing it won't matter anyways.

"Just uncomfortable. I don't do small talk, or much talking at all with people I don't know." I down the rest of the beer and quickly grab another one.

"Yea, I've noticed," London says sarcastically. Then, she smiles, nearly knocking the breath right out of me. How the hell does she do that? "But you're better at it than you think. Besides, these people are some of the best. If you treat them right, they'll treat you right. And they don't do small talk either." She winks.

If we were anywhere but here right now, I'd have her up against the wall in less than a second. Since that's not exactly possible and I'd prefer to not have an audience, I settle for leaning in and kissing her on the cheek. It's nowhere near the same, but it'll do for now.

"You don't have to convince me. I'm already here." I say smirking.

"I know. I just want you to relax and enjoy yourself."

"The only way that's going to happen is if I have several more of these," I state, holding up the beer in my hand.

"Mom," Brayden yells as he rushes up to us, barely stopping before running into London.

"Woah, kid, where's the fire?" I ask.

He quirks his brows, tilting his head to me. "What?"

"Never mind," I laugh, shaking my head.

He turns back to London. "Can Hannah and I swim in the pool?"

The little red-headed girl from earlier bounces up and down next to him. "Please, Aunt London. We promise we'll be careful," she begs excitedly.

"If your mom and dad are okay with it, then that's fine. Just make sure you change into your swim trunks first, B."

He rolls his eyes. "I know, Mom. I'm not stupid." Turning to me quickly, he asks, "Wanna swim with us Mr. Jamie?"

His eyes shine up at me expectantly. Guess, it's a good thing I brought a swimsuit with me. "I'd love to."

Besides, it's the perfect way to avoid the personal conversations bound to happen at the table with the adults.

I follow Brayden to the car, grabbing the bags from the back and head inside to change. He points me to a bathroom, then heads off in the opposite direction to change. When I'm done, I slip the bag on my shoulders and step out of the bathroom. I cross the hall and lean against the far wall, facing the direction Brayden took off in.

"If you're waiting on the kids, they're already in the pool." A voice says behind me.

I turn to see Ki's boyfriend, Hunter, just inside the kitchen, a cold beer in his hand. "Ah, thanks." I nod in his direction, pushing off the wall and making my way around Hunter and to the back door.

"I think it's great London found you. She deserves to have someone who loves her and makes her happy." His words stop me in my tracks. Love? What is he talking about?

"You might not know it yet, but I can see it in the way you

218

look at her. It's the same way I look at my girl, like I'd be nothing without her."

I don't move, instead I stare down at the door handle. "I don't..." I pause, not sure how to finish my statement. Anything I say would be a lie. I know that.

"You can run from your feelings all you want to, but it won't change them. Trust me on that one. It's what I did with Ki, but when you find the right person, those feelings never go away, no matter how fast you run from them. Sometimes, it's better to just accept the way you feel," he states, and I hear the tap of his shoes on the hardwood floor as he leaves the kitchen.

I stand there, the door handle becoming a blur as my eyes remain fixed on it. I don't love her. I can't love her.

But what if I do?

She's making me start to wonder if I have more to offer than a good time, maybe I'm not as broken as I think.

Twenty-Nine

London

I sit in the lounger next to Ki and Sabrina, sipping on the cold beer in my hand. Jamie and Brayden splash in the pool in front of us, a tiny Hannah floating on a large pink floatie like the little princess she is. I can't help but stare at Jamie as he splashes Brayden, his strong shoulder muscles clenching and releasing with the movement.

Awe, the things he can do to me with those muscles. Shit, the things he can do to me in general. Just thinking about it gets me all hot and bothered.

"You look happy," Ki states, her hand settled on her stomach.

I feel her eyes on me before I glance her way. She has a sneaky smile on her face that says she knows something I don't know.

Hell, maybe she does.

"Jamie is pretty great, which makes it easy to be happy."

My smile falters as I think about all the ways this is bound to go wrong like the fact that he could decide to go back to his celebrity lifestyle and I'm not sure I want to be a part of it or the fact he still has so much to work through about the accident. Lately, it's been harder and harder to ignore these worries no matter how hard I try.

Sabrina studies me, her face full of questions that I'm pretty sure I can't answer. "So, what's your deal?" she asks simply.

I know what she's getting at, but I'd rather not answer. "What do you mean?"

"Are you guys dating or what?"

Her question hits me in the gut. I don't know what we are or what to call us, but it sure feels like dating to me. Except we've had this conversation, and this isn't dating according to him. At least, not the dating that involves feelings. He's made that pretty clear with all his proclamations about how he can't give me anything but sex.

I'm not sure I really want to share that with the girls though.

Besides, after everything he told me the other night, it feels even more real. I mean the man finally told me what happened to him to make him so messed up, and all I wanted to do was hold him tight and take his pain away.

So, what does that say about us? Or me? Honestly, it's probably just me with these feelings because that's the kind of person I am. Always falling for the guys I can't have or not falling for them in general. Clearly, that depends on the day and my mood.

"I don't know what to call us," I finally admit, sighing with defeat. "He says he can't give me more than sex, but the other day, he finally opened up to me. It made this whole thing feel so much more intense."

I'm glad he's far enough away from us and them playing in the pool is loud enough that he can't hear what we're saying.

Sabrina's eyebrows pop up and her face looks way too giddy. "You mean to tell me you are doing the whole friends with benefits thing with the hot, hunky celebrity staying at your hotel?"

"I mean, I wouldn't call it that," I deny, hiding my face in my beer and shrugging my shoulders.

She eyes me curiously. "But that's what it is."

"No, it's not."

"Are you having sex?"

I nod, a blush creeping to my cheeks at her unnecessarily invasive question.

"Are you hanging out?"

"Yes, but as friends. We went to the fun park and rode golf carts one day with Brayden."

Ki snickers, and I zero a glare in on her. She waves me off. "What? Am I not allowed to enjoy this?"

"No," I mutter, turning back to Sabrina who's tapping a finger on her chin.

"Do you go out on dates?"

I shake my head and give her a dumbfounded look. She already knows the answers to these questions.

"Then, my dear, you are friends with benefits," she insists.

"Fine, maybe we are. Is there something wrong with that?"

Sabrina shakes her head. "Not a damn thing. Other than the fact that I wish it was me."

I stare at the beer in my hand, running my fingers up and down the condensation on the can. It's funny that no matter how many times I clear it away, it always seems to come back. Kind of like my feelings.

I feel eyes on me, but I don't look up. I know Ki and Sabrina are studying me, trying to figure out how I feel about Jamie and what I think about the situation. It's a shame staring at me won't help. I've gotten way too good at hiding how I truly feel about him.

"You're in love with him, aren't you?" Ki blurts, and I nearly choke on my own spit.

Am I in love with him?

I've never been in love. I'm not even sure I really know what it is. My mom and I didn't exactly have the best relationship growing up, and love wasn't really part of her vocabulary. Besides, she worked all the time.

She said that was to make sure we had a place to live and food on the table, but sometimes I wondered if it was so she didn't have to spend time with me - the reminder that her husband didn't want her anymore.

None of that matters though because I'm not in love. At least, I think I'm not, but maybe I am. Shit, I don't know. I know I like him. Really, really like him. We have fun, he does nice things, he cares for my son...blah, blah, blah. And the other night, I felt his pain as mine. I wanted to rip every tragic memory from his mind so he never had to relive them again.

But that's not love. Is it?

Or maybe it is?

One thing I know for sure is the thought of him leaving, not being a part of our lives, scares the daylights out of me. I don't know if I could handle that kind of goodbye from him.

"Is it bad that I'm not sure?" I ask cautiously, semi-afraid of their answers.

"Of course not." Sabrina waves off my comment. "I've never been sure." Her tone is casual, making it sound like it's completely normal to not know if you're in love with someone.

"Are you unsure or afraid?" Ki's eyes meet mine, and I blow out a breath. "Sometimes our fear convinces us that we're not sure when deep down we know how we really feel."

"Is that what happened with you and Hunter?" I ask, pretty sure I already know the answer. The fear was always clear on her face, but so was the love... whether she'd wanted to admit it or not.

"Kind of, yes. I mean, I was definitely afraid, more than necessary, and I think it made me unsure if what I felt for him was real or not." Ki sips casually on her bottle of water.

How do these girls make all of this seem so - I don't know - normal? Cause none of this feels normal. I feel like I should know if it's love, not be confused as hell.

"I am a little afraid," I admit. "But the fear stems more from not knowing where we stand now, and what will happen when it's time for him to go home."

Damn, maybe I am in love with him already. I wouldn't possibly be this afraid if I wasn't, and the thought of him leaving wouldn't put a crack in my heart the way it does now.

My eyes widen, and I groan. "Damn, you're right. I am in love with him."

Needing to do something other than dwell on this newfound revelation, I pull the beer to my lips and chug. My heart pounds against my chest as the cool liquid slides down my throat like a waterfall.

What the hell?

I knew this was going to happen. I should have kept to myself and stayed away from Jamie, but that was easier said than done. Chemistry with someone is no joke. The force between us was too damn strong for me to fight.

A squeal catches my attention, and my gaze drifts back to the pool. Jamie and Brayden are playing some kind of game, chasing each other through the water.

My heart stops pounding so hard, and warmth rolls over me like a crashing wave. I never thought I'd see my son having moments like these. A weird mixture of panic and happiness fills my soul.

I'm in too deep. Brayden is in too deep. And there's not a damn thing I can do to fix it.

"I don't think that's a bad thing," Ki's voice tugs me out of my thoughts and back to the present.

"You don't?"

She tips her head towards the pool. "Look at him. What do you see?"

I see his muscles strain against his skin as he lifts Brayden up and tosses him back into the water. His eyes crinkle at the sides with a smile when Brayden pushes through the water back at him.

My lips turn up just as Jamie meets my gaze. His heated eyes connect with mine, and his grin nearly knocks the air from my lungs. He literally takes my breath away, and I know that's not normal. He's the only man who has ever been able to do that to me.

"That's not the face of a guy with no feelings for you," Ki whispers beside me.

"Definitely not," Sabrina agrees. "That's the face of a guy who's smitten with you, not using you for sex."

I can't deny the excitement that flutters in my stomach or the way my heart beats a little livelier. I don't know everything about Jamie, but I do know he'd never hurt me. Not on purpose anyway.

Besides, at this point, I can't really back out. I've already given into my feelings, let them take over. Maybe he will hurt me. Maybe he will surprise me. Either way, I don't think I can do much

else than keep enjoying the time I have with him.
Even if it ends with nothing but heartbreak.

Thirty

Jamie

So, maybe the barbecue and socializing wasn't all that bad. After playing in the pool with the kids, we all gathered round the patio to eat. Laughter filled the table as easy conversation flowed between all of us. I even got along really well with Ki's boyfriend, Hunter.

"Did you see that one cannonball I did? The splash was so big that it soaked Hannah across the pool. She was so mad," Brayden tells us from the backseat of the car as we head back to their house.

"No, I missed that," London says, never taking her eyes off the road.

She had far less to drink than I did, and I'm glad she thought about who'd be driving us home. I was far more concerned about drowning my nerves to think about that.

"Awe, I wish you'd seen it. It was so cool. Right, Mr. Jamie?"

"Right," I confirm, chuckling. I've told him he can stop calling me Mr. Jamie, but he hasn't stopped yet.

"So, Jamie, was it as bad as you'd expected it to be?" London asks, glancing over at me with a sarcastic smirk on her lips.

"No, it wasn't too bad I suppose."

"You suppose?"

"I'm just playing. It was a lot better than I expected it to be. I don't know why small things like that make me so nervous."

"Yea, that surprised me too."

"I think it's all the bad experiences with fans I've had over the years," I admit, running my hands along my scruffy beard.

"I guess you probably have to deal with a lot of crazy people that make social situations difficult."

"Yea, I do." I peek in the rear-view mirror, seeing a passed-out Brayden in the back seat. "Guess today wore him out?"

If I'm being honest, today wore me out, too. Who knew spending the whole day playing with kids could make a person so exhausted? And where the hell do they get all this energy from?

"Yea, he always passes out in the car after we leave Ki's place. He's not used to spending all that time running around."

"I think it's wonderful that you and your friends get together like that," I admit after a moment of silence.

In my line of business, moments like that are few and far between. Everything is built for show, to make you look good. Nothing is ever genuine, not even the news stories about the bad things. Even those are filled with half-truths. Damon always says they'll do anything for a good story.

"What do you mean?" she asks, shifting in her seat as we inch closer to her house.

"You know? You all get together and genuinely have a good time. It's easy to see that your friends actually care about you and each other."

She pulls into the driveway, puts the car in park, and turns to look at me. "I spent my whole childhood searching for friends like that, the ones that felt like family. My own family wasn't exactly the one with moments like that," she pauses, glancing away from me like she's embarrassed to admit that.

"Not all families are the picture-perfect ones. You know my life wasn't like that. It's just the way it goes sometimes." I lift her chin with my finger, pulling her eyes back to mine.

She sighs heavily, like she wants to tell me what's going through her mind, but she's hesitant, too. The desire to tell me must win out because she sucks in a deep breath and speaks, "My childhood wasn't exactly pleasant. Don't get me wrong, I had fun, but my mom worked all the time. And my grandparents never really wanted anything to do with me. The only reason they let us live with them was because they felt like it was their fault their daughter got married and pregnant so young and her husband walked out on her. I can't even begin to tell you how many times I was told I was a mistake growing up.

"I mean, imagine living with that pressure. I knew my mom loved me in her own way and as I got older, we grew closer. But nothing was going to be normal between us. We were never going to have the kind of relationship I have with B. In a way, I think she resented me for making her life what it was."

London's words fall on my ears, and I can't help the way my chest tightens. I can't imagine ever growing up in a house where I felt that unwanted. Even after my parents died, I never felt that way. My grandma always told me how grateful she was for me and how much she loved me.

"I can't even imagine," I say, not sure what else to add.

"Because you didn't have a family like that," she states nonchalantly.

"No, I didn't." My voice is soft and deep as I think of any way possible to erase this pain from London's life. Even if it were possible for me to do, I'm not sure she'd want me to. Something tells me that her childhood is what made her into the strong, resilient woman she is today. And honestly, I wouldn't want to change that about her at all. It's one of the things I love about her.

Love?

Did I just say I *love* that about her?

I glance out the window, staring up into the black sky, glittering with millions of stars. I let out a few deep breaths, close my eyes, and dwell on that simple four-letter word. What does it mean that it came out when thinking about her?

Hell if I know. I thought that part of me was dead - the part that could feel anything remotely different from guilt and despair. Maybe I was wrong? Maybe it wasn't entirely dead, but close enough to make me feel like it. Maybe London brought it back to life?

I'm pretty damn sure that London has done more than she could ever realize in bringing me out of the darkness. Although, I must admit, the therapist helped a lot too.

I chuckle to myself, *damn it all to hell, Hunter was right.*

"What are you thinking about?" London breaks the brief moment of silence.

I don't know how to respond because a million things are running through my mind as I stare into the dark abyss in front of me. And I'm not sure I should tell her about the thing at the forefront of all those thoughts: her.

None of this was supposed to happen. I wasn't supposed to catch feelings, and I honestly didn't think I had until Hunter brought it up at the party. He mentioned that he could see how I felt about London in the way I looked at her and how he was the same way with Ki. If he hadn't run from his feelings, he said his life would have turned out so much differently.

I wonder if it was some kind of psychic thing he was doing

because it felt like he was reading my mind. How could he possibly know that the idea of running away had crossed my mind when I realized what he said was true?

"Jamie?" London questions gently.

I look her way, her face glowing in the moonlight and streetlamps shining through the window. She looks gorgeous even after such a long, tiring day. How does she manage to do that?

I cup my hands around her rosy cheeks and whisper, "You are beautiful, inside and out."

She laughs, brushing off my words and pulling away from me uncomfortably. "Thank you," she says. "And thank you for coming today. I'm pretty sure you made Brayden's year."

"I had so much fun with him. He's such a great kid."

She moves her head to look at the backseat, her eyes landing on her sleeping son while mine remain locked on her face. A tornado of emotions sweep across her features, and I feel the tug to wrap my arms around her. I don't move though. Something tells me that's not what she needs right now.

"He loves you," she mutters solemnly, and her words pull at my heartstrings. I know what she's thinking as she says them. I'm going to leave eventually, and it's going to hurt him.

Shit. How did I let things get this far with them?

Because you enjoyed having something to live for again. You enjoyed being part of a family.

I shake the thoughts from my head. Even if they are true, this isn't my family or my home.

"And not just because you're his favorite movie star," she continues. "You pay attention to him. You treat him the way a father treats a son. He never had that. And I hate his father for taking that kind of relationship away from him."

Her eyes peer up at me, tears encasing their outer edges. Her sadness pierces my heart and makes it hard for me to breathe. I process her words and my mind floats to Hunter. They seemed to get along great, and Brayden clearly loves him. "What about Hunter?" I ask.

A sad smile pulls on her now tense face. "That's a long story, but he's only been part of his life recently. And it's not really the same. Hunter is just getting to know his daughter, and they have another on the way. He's so focused on his family, but I don't blame him. Their relationship hasn't exactly been a party."

"I don't think anyone's is a party, not really. I mean mine sure as hell haven't been."

"Mine either," she huffs out a sharp laugh. "Why does everything in life have to be so damn hard? I feel like I keep waiting for that moment when I finally reach the top of the mountain I've been climbing for far too long, but it never seems to come."

The image hits me hard, and I know exactly what she means. Only lately, I haven't been moving up the mountain. No, I've been on some kind of treadmill type thing. No matter how many steps I take, I seem to stay in the same place.

Well, that was until I met her. My eyes land on her oval-shaped face. Her pert nose and her soft plush lips stand out. Every moment we've spent together up to this point flashes across my mind. Her smile leaves a fiery trail in its wake. Her luscious curves leave me begging for more every damn time. And her sweet, yet desperately independent, personality seems to drag me up that hill with her.

For the first time, it occurs to me that I'm not so stuck anymore. I'm nowhere near the same man I was when I first stepped in Sunrise. And I know London is a big part of that.

I reach for her hand across the center console. "I know exactly what you mean, but maybe we were both just waiting for someone to come along and help us carry the load."

She quirks her brows at me and smirks. "You think I can't carry the load on my own?"

I can't tell if she's joking or being serious. My eyes dart around the darkness of the car, avoiding hers, but I can feel the heat of her gaze sending daggers into my skin.

"That's not what I meant," I croak, clearing my throat and gathering my thoughts. "I just think maybe we aren't meant to carry the burdens of life on our own. Maybe we're meant to share them with someone else to make it easier to climb that mountain. Besides, I don't think there's anything about *us* that's hard." I wink.

"Except maybe your, you know," she giggles, pointing her eyes towards my crotch.

"Yea, maybe except that," I agree, just before claiming her

lips with mine.

Thirty-One
London

Maybe we needed someone to help us carry the load.

Those words reverberate in my mind for the weeks to come. Even now, in the middle of October, those words find me second guessing everything I've ever thought about this life.

I didn't know what to say to him after he said that. The feminist in me wanted to be angry, but the tired single mother understood.

I've always looked at a lover as just that - there to satisfy my needs. Did I want a husband? Yes, of course. Did I want to fall in love? Absolutely, but not because I wanted a partner to help me through life. I just wanted someone to spend time with, but maybe Jamie's right.

Maybe your partner isn't there to simply be your friend and do things with you, but to help you carry the load of your burdens as well as theirs. I mean it is easier to carry a heavy piece of furniture with two people rather than on your own. Maybe that's the same thing for life, too.

I won't lie, it's been nice having someone to talk to, to lean on even though I haven't relied on him for much. Part of that's because of my independent nature, and the other part is because of the expiration date he put on us from the start.

Even with that though, he's around a lot and loves to hang out with Brayden. They always seem to be playing some kind of game together or watching movies or swapping stories.

Not to mention, I've come to enjoy the fact that my bed doesn't feel so empty anymore, especially since he's in it pretty much all the time now. It started a week or two ago when he came over for dinner, and he just never seemed to leave. If I'm being honest, I didn't want him to leave. Correction: I *don't* want him to leave.

We've definitely moved from "just sex" to something more, whether we've defined it or not. And as much as I want a definition of us, I also don't want to ruin what this has become either.

It's so hard for me to believe I've only known him a couple months. He feels so much like part of our family.

But I can't think like that, no matter how much it feels that way or how much I love it, because I can't deny that he might leave for another movie or head back to Hollywood.

I can't admit it.

I *won't* admit it.

Not even when he took Brayden and I to a baseball game last week, and we had the best possible seats. Or when he made known that I was his by placing a protective hand around my waist as some drunk jackass tried to take me home. Or when he took us to the pumpkin patch and helped Brayden find the biggest pumpkin to carve for Halloween.

No, I didn't admit it then. And I sure as hell will not admit it now. Because if I'm falling for him that means Brayden is too, and that will make it so much harder when it's time for Jamie to go home.

Soft footsteps pad along the tile floor just outside my doorway, and my heart rate picks up as I glance at the clock.

He's right on time, just like he has been every day since the first lunch he brought me. He said he has nothing better to do and insisted on joining me for lunch every day since.

"Hey," he says in that deep voice I love so much. Never mind the fact it brought goosebumps to my skin or wet my panties, which honestly seemed to be an all-the-time thing since we've met.

"Hi," I say, smiling up at him and pushing the paperwork in front of me to the side.

He steps into my office and places a brown paper bag from Sunrise Cafe on the desk in front of me, taking his usual seat.

"How's your day?" he asks, leaning back in the metal chair and moving around to get comfortable. "You'd think this damn thing would get more comfortable the more I sit in it, but you'd be wrong," he says, his mouth contorted in disgust.

I point to the chair. "I mean it is hard and metal with zero cushions on it. Did you really expect it to be comfortable?" I ask, snickering behind my hand.

He eyes me with disdain. "No, but a man can dream."

"And that's what you choose to dream about?"

Clouds of desire gather in his eyes, sending electric shocks of lightning through my body.

Will this feeling ever get old? Somehow, I highly doubt it, and yet, knowing my luck with men, it will.

"I dream about a lot of things, and I can guarantee you that this chair is definitely not one of them," his voice is thick with lust and his eyes burn my skin, making me wish my office were a little farther away from the front desk.

Heat burns my cheeks at the thought, and it flows down to my neck and chest like it always does when I get nervous or heated.

I clear my throat and hastily change the subject before I do something completely irrational. I may want to pounce on this man like a wild lioness, but I need to keep my job more. "So, what have you been up to today?"

He shakes his head. "Not too much. Just the usual. Do you still need me to meet Brayden at the house today at 3?"

"Yes, that would be perfect. Sabrina said she can't make it, and Ki has to do something with her dad this evening."

"Got it," he says, saluting me.

"And don't make plans for dinner tonight. I plan to repay you with dinner."

"I've already told you that you don't have to repay me for anything," he insists, his tall frame pulling the chair closer to the desk and me.

The screeching of metal on tile makes me shiver. "Gah, I really hate that sound, almost as much as fingernails on a chalkboard."

"Me too, but I couldn't help it." He laughs, moving the chair this time by picking it up and setting it back down. "Better?"

"Much better." I smile and reach into the bag in front of me. "So, what do we have for lunch today?"

"Not a clue," he says, his lips in a confused line. "All Ki said was that it's your favorite."

"*Yess*," I hiss in excitement. I know exactly what it is, and I love that Ki knew to make it for me today. It's like she can read my mind.

Jamie leans forward, his elbows resting on his knees and his eyes studying the paper bag in front of him as I rustle around inside. "I feel like with the amount of time we spend together I should know what your favorite sandwich is, yet I have no idea," he says, giving me a perplexed look.

I pull the takeout boxes from the bag and open the one with my name on it, slowly, savoring the aromas of ham, cheese, and basil.

Jamie stares at the sandwich as pesto sauce slides down my hand. "Is that pesto on a grilled ham and cheese sandwich?" he asks, his face crinkling with disgust.

"Mhm," I respond, lifting the multi-grain bread to my lips and taking a delicate bite. I moan as the tantalizing flavors hit my tongue. "This sandwich is way better than any old grilled cheese," I state firmly.

The sour look plastered on Jamie's face tells me he very much disagrees with that statement. "I beg to differ. Pesto sauce does not belong on a grilled cheese," he insists, shaking his head and looking a little green in the face. Or maybe that's my imagination?

"The only reason you think that is because you haven't tried it," I argue, holding out half of the sandwich for him to try.

He snaps his mouth shut and refuses to take it no matter how many times I wiggle the sandwich in front of him. "You can stop that. I'm not putting that abomination in my mouth."

I pull the sandwich back protectively and pout. "How dare you call this delectable dish an abomination!" I say, feigning shock.

If Jamie ever had any doubts about my sanity, this moment would confirm them. I'm a weirdo.

He chuckles. "Life is never boring with you."

"Would you rather it be boring?" I ask around a bite of sandwich.

"Hell no, boring sucks and isn't nearly as fun." He winks, and I'm not sure if he's talking about life in general or sex. One thing I do know is neither of them are boring with him.

Thirty-Two

Jamie

There's not a damn thing I would change about London. Absolutely nothing. Not her quirky personality, or her undeniable love and compassion for everyone around her.

Not even the fact that she likes pesto sauce on her grilled cheese sandwich.

That realization should scare the fuck out of me, but for some reason, it doesn't.

The gentle sea breeze swims around me as I walk through Sunrise on my way to London's house. Even though it's officially fall, the salty ocean air still feels warm and humid, causing me to sweat in the most inconvenient places.

It doesn't matter though because for the first time in months, I'm actually happy. I'm at peace. Do the memories still grab me at times? Yes, but the therapy sessions have really helped me learn how to deal with them when they do. Not to mention, being with London and growing closer to her each day has given me something to look forward too.

The therapist says these emotions and memories won't ever completely go away but learning how to manage them and how to relax when they take over can help me feel more normal again. So far, she's been right. Whenever I feel the waves crashing down, I close my eyes and think about what makes me happy, what gives me purpose - London and Brayden. Then, I count to ten and take several deep breaths until I feel myself finding my way back to reality.

I'd never admit this to Damon, but he was right the whole time.

As I continue walking through downtown, my phone vibrates in my back pocket.

Speak of the devil. I sigh, answering the phone with the click of a button. "Yes," I grunt, a little annoyed that my thoughts have been interrupted.

"Good to talk to you, too," Damon says sarcastically.

"Sorry, I'm just a little busy at the moment," I lie, even though it's not a *complete* lie. I am busy - thinking about the woman that's somehow managed to capture my damn heart and all the ways I don't feel so broken anymore.

"With what? You don't exactly have anything to do in Sunrise."

I'm not sure what to say to him. He knows about London, but he doesn't know just how close we've gotten over the last few months. Our conversations have generally been brief and business-focused because frankly, I didn't want his opinion on whatever this thing is between us.

If I'm being honest, I didn't want him to tell me exactly what I already know - I'm in love with her.

There. I said it.

I went into this whole thing telling her I couldn't give her more than sex, and she agreed to it. Now, here I am admitting that I love her.

How insane does that make me look?

I'm the one who set the damn rules in the first place, and the thought of even telling London how I feel makes me want to run as far away as possible. I can't imagine that those three words won't terrify her to death. I mean she did agree to this being a purely sexual relationship.

Although, she has been a major part of making this more than that by inviting me over to dinner every night or asking me to stay after we fuck each other's brains out or by taking me to barbecues with her friends.

Maybe she wouldn't be as freaked out as I think she would be, but that doesn't make me less afraid of telling her. I know London better now, and I know that she doesn't jump into things without thinking them through. That means she thought long and hard about it before agreeing to only sex, and I think that's the part that terrifies me the most. If she made that decision so firmly, is there any room to change her mind and make her see that we should be more?

"Earth to Jameson, are you still there or did you hang up on me again?" Damon's voice carries loudly through the phone.

"No, I'm still here," I say, annoyance filling my tone.

Maybe I should hang up on him so I can continue thinking about all of this.

"Good, I need to talk to you about some business stuff, but first, how are you doing?"

"I'm alright," I pause, debating whether or not I should mention London and my newfound feelings.

"How're things with that girl?"

I guess that settles my debate. I suck in a deep breath and exhale slowly, formulating the words I want to say. I don't know if I want to reveal too much to my friend, but also, I know it would be nice to voice this with a real person.

"Actually, they're going really well."

"Oh really?" His tone piques with curiosity.

Maybe I shouldn't say anything more about it? Shit, I hate being this indecisive. I'm never like this. I've always known what I want and never been afraid to make it happen. Why has that changed so much since being in Sunrise?

The accident, my brain reminds me.

Right, as if I could forget about that, and yet for a moment, I actually did. Nothing about me has been the same since the accident no matter how much I wish it were. Shit, I can't even make simple decisions without second guessing myself. It's almost like I don't even trust myself to do the right thing.

"Fuck, I don't know," I say, my nostrils flaring with unwanted anger.

"What?" Damon asks, a clear tone of confusion in his voice.

"I don't know," I repeat, harsher and slower this time.

"I get that, but what don't you know?"

"Anything. Everything. Fuck, Damon, I think I love her, and I don't know what to do with that. I made a promise to myself after the accident that I would never allow myself to love again. I took that family's symbol of love away. I didn't think I deserved to be happy or feel love."

"But you know that's not true."

"Do I?" I yell. I know it makes me look volatile and crazy on the street. People stare at me as I make my way through downtown and onto the side street London lives on.

"Yes, you do. I know you're mad at yourself for making that mistake and hurting that family, but you didn't do it on purpose. You didn't go out driving that night, planning to run into that family and kill their daughter. It was an honest to God accident. And I know you know that." Damon's voice screeches through the phone fiercely.

His words assault me in a way that none ever have before, and for the first time, I'm thinking about the fact that it *was* an accident. I'm looking at the entire situation as if I never meant it to happen rather than blaming myself for it. Maybe I can't fully accept that I didn't do it on purpose right this instant, but maybe with time?

"I just..." my words fall off, and I don't know what else to say to him.

His voice is soft when he speaks again. "Jamie, you know I love you like a brother. You're not just my client. You're my best friend. But this isn't a good look on you. Not to mention, studios and producers are starting to pull out on movie deals because of how you've reacted since the accident.

"However, I do know that since you started seeing a counselor, you've been more like your old self again. You've even, dare I say it, been happy. I know you're mad at yourself and scared that you might destroy another family, but you won't. Just because you had one accident, doesn't mean you're bound to destroy everything you touch from here on out. Not to mention, you sought out help. You're working through everything. That's all you can do, that and live."

He sighs, and I realize that I'm now standing outside London's house.

"I guess all I'm trying to say is it's okay to let yourself fall in love and feel this way."

I hear his words, I do, but I feel them even more. They go all the way to my core, to the deepest recesses of my mind.

It's okay to be in love with London. It's okay to let myself feel this kind of happiness again. The therapist has told me that in every session, but it's hard for me to take that step, to allow myself something I believed I didn't deserve for so long.

Thirty-Three
London

I know I don't have to go all out for dinner tonight, but I can't help it. I could think of a thousand ways to show my appreciation to Jamie for everything he's done for Brayden and me, but nothing says thank you quite like my famous chicken pot pie and homemade peach cobbler.

Although, I'm pretty sure Jamie would disagree. In fact, I think he'd say sex is a much better way to say thank you, but if I've learned anything from the great women of the South, it's that food is the only true way to say anything.

I grab a grocery cart on my way into the store, planning to

make this as quick a trip as possible, as I only need a few things. There's a buzzing excitement that keeps me energized as I enter the store and a smile plastered on my face as I think about dinner with my boys.

Yes, my boys – that's what I'm calling Jamie and Brayden because that's exactly what they are to me. I've accepted the cold, hard truth that Jamie is a part of me for however long he's here.

I push the cart towards the produce section, picking out the veggies I need for inside the pot pie. Then, I head to the meat area where I grab the chicken, until I'm in the dairy section.

Butter, heavy whipping cream, and more milk. I'm staring at the different kinds of milk and balking at the prices when I see…

No way, it cannot be possible. My eyes land on the one man I haven't seen in almost a decade, and frankly, never wanted to see again.

Heat immediately pulses to my cheeks, and anger runs through my veins. I stare at him, shooting daggers at his back as he pushes a cart with two little boys, I assume his children, inside it.

This cannot be happening. My child wasn't good enough for him, but whatever whore he slept with after me was? I want to scream and cuss him out, throw the celery and carrots at his head, but I don't. Instead, I squeeze the handle of the cart so tight my knuckles turn white.

I need to get out of here before he sees me. Not that he'd recognize me if he did. I don't have the same mousy features I had back then. I'm stronger, and my skin is more weathered than it used to be, thanks to all the fighting I've had to do to give my son the best life possible.

I turn my cart around and head the opposite direction. I round the end of the aisle and find myself face to face with him. *Shit!*

"London?" His eyes search mine and his brows crinkle together.

"Hamish," I say curtly, averting my gaze from his face.

"It's been a long time," his voice is soft, deep, but it doesn't have the same effect on me as it did in the past.

"Mhm, by no choice of mine," I spit out, my eyes landing on the two boys in front of me. "I see you have a new family." I nod to the two boys fighting with each other over who gets to hold the cereal box.

He sighs, his eyes dropping to the boys. "Look, I'm sorry," I don't let him finish before I cut him off.

"Please don't. I don't need your apologies. We're fine without you. As you so clearly stated that night, my bastard child and I never needed you." I squeeze the handle on the grocery cart until my knuckles turn white.

"London," he starts, but I don't stay to listen. I need to get out of here, away from him, away from the man that didn't think me or my son were good enough for him.

I push the cart furiously around Hamish and head as fast as I can to the checkout lane. I hurry to place my items on the conveyor belt and pray like hell he doesn't follow me. The last thing I need is for Hamish to continue whatever that conversation was and start asking questions about our son, like he has a right to know him after dumping us all those years ago.

Hell, I don't even know if he'd want anything to do with us at this point, but I'm not taking any chances.

No, I'm getting the hell out of dodge as quickly as I can.

Once I've paid for everything and the bags are tucked back in my cart, I make my way out to the car, unloading the bags into the trunk quickly. I furiously march the cart over to the return and practically run back to the car.

I slam the door shut and take a deep breath, letting out all the tension that's built up in my shoulders. I relax now that I'm in the safety of my old beat-up Honda. I know without a shadow of a doubt that jackass won't come near this disgrace of a car.

I pull out of the parking lot and head home. It only takes five minutes before I'm pulling into my driveway.

Brayden rushes out the front door and straight into my arms. Tears prick at the corner of my eyes as I think that this is exactly what I needed after that trip to the store. Jamie follows closely behind, leaning in to give me a kiss on the cheek and looking at me curiously.

"Everything okay?" he asks, softly.

"Yea, I'm all good," I say, knowing I don't sound convincing at all.

"Here, let Brayden and I get the groceries. You go ahead

inside."

Normally, I'd argue about how a woman can just as easily carry the groceries in the house, but honestly, I need the moment of privacy to process what just happened.

I slip through the front door, leaving the boys to the groceries and head straight to the kitchen. The kitchen is my happy place, as crazy as that sounds. It's the one place that allows me to think and relax all at the same time. I don't know if it's because it keeps my hands busy and my mind moving or what, but I've always loved the way cooking makes me feel.

I start pulling out the utensils, bowls, and pans I'll need to make dinner and can't help the way my mind instantly goes to Brayden's father. I move through the motions without even realizing what I'm doing. All I can see in front of me is his face, how happy he looked pushing his children through the grocery store. The children he decided to keep while he brushed my son away.

I always wondered if this day would come, if I'd run into him. I'd hoped he'd never come back here after what he did, but clearly that was too much to hope for.

Thank God Brayden wasn't with me. Not that he'd have known who the man was since he's never met him.

But what if Hamish had recognized me while I was in there and Brayden had been with me? I don't even want to think about how that would have gone over.

"Here ya go, Mom," Brayden's voice breaks through my fog

of thoughts as he places the grocery bags on the counter alongside Jamie.

I begin laying out what I need on the counter. I empty all the bags and realize I didn't even get the items from the dairy section. "Shit," I mutter, placing the last of the items on the counter.

Jamie comes around the island and leans into my ear. "What's wrong?"

"I forgot the butter, cream, and milk," I say, almost in tears.

He rubs his hands up and down my arms, reassuring me. "Where are your keys? Brayden and I will run out and get it. You look like you need a moment anyway."

I nod, choking back a sob. I don't want to cry, but I know it's inevitable. I just want to wait until they're both gone before I let it all out. "They're on the hook by the door."

He kisses me on the cheek before walking out of the kitchen. "B, let's run to the store real quick," he hollers.

As the front door slams shut, the dam on my tears breaks loose, and I fall to the ground, sobbing. I lean against the cabinets, the hardwood floors cold against my thighs as I let out every single tear of frustration and hate.

And hate that man, I do. I hate him with every fiber of my being. He left my son without a father all because he's a selfish ass.

Then, Jamie's face flashes in my mind. His kind eyes and caring attitude stare back at me. Images of him playing catch with Brayden, helping him with homework, and playing games with him in the pool flood my brain until a sense of calm and warmth flows through me.

Forget that selfish asshole, Brayden never needed him anyway, and he sure as hell doesn't need him now. Jamie is far better to him than Hamish ever would have been.

Thirty-Four
Jamie

I don't know what's going on with London. I'm sure it's nothing, but that doesn't keep my heart from racing or the panic setting in. I've never seen her so worked up or in such a frenzy.

She was fine when I left her at lunch, happy and smiling. Then, she gets home from the store, and she's so pale. She looks like she's seen a ghost. I wanted to help her, but I had no idea what to do.

I just felt like she needed some space. Going to the store with Brayden seemed like the best way to give that to her, so that's exactly why I offered to go when she realized she forgot some things.

I look in the rear view of London's beat up old Honda,

checking to make sure Brayden is buckled in. "You ready to go?"

He nods his head, but his face is solemn, almost as if he's concerned about something. "You alright, buddy?" I decide to ask before pulling out onto the road. I don't need anything distracting me while I drive, especially not with Brayden in the car and especially since I haven't driven in months.

He leans his head in his hand, looking out the window thoughtfully. "Is my mom okay? She didn't seem like herself."

No, she didn't seem like herself, and I'm glad I wasn't the only one to pick up on it, even if Brayden's frowning face is killing me.

I turn around in my seat so I'm facing him the best I can. Luckily, he chose to sit on the back passenger side, making it a lot easier. "Honestly, I don't know, kid."

He glances at me, his eyes red around the rims like he wants to cry. "Do you think it's something I did?"

"What? No. Why would you think that?" I ask, my heart breaking a little more.

"I got in trouble at school today. They sent me to the principal's office and everything. What if my mom was mad at me for getting in trouble? I never get in trouble." His voice sounds so small and scared.

I twist a little more in the driver's seat, looking him directly in the eye. "Listen to me, B. You are not a bad kid or the reason your mom is upset. I think something else happened today to make your mom sad, but whatever it was you did wasn't it. Your mom loves you, and she knows you're a good kid."

"But what if what I did was really bad?"

"What did you do? Want to talk to me about it?"

"I hurt someone. They wouldn't leave me alone. They kept making fun of me, and it made me so angry. I couldn't help it. I just hit them in the stomach." Tears roll down his cheeks, and I never knew watching this kid cry could hurt me more than anything else in the world.

I can't stay in this spot for the rest of this conversation. This is something I need to do face to face. I climb out of the car and walk around the back to Brayden's door. Pulling it open, I bend down to his level and look him straight in the eyes.

"I'm not saying that it's okay to hit someone, B, but it also wasn't okay for that kid to bully you either. Could you have done things different? Yes, we can always do things differently, but sometimes it doesn't matter how careful we are, things still happen. But your mother would never stop loving you or be mad at you for standing up for yourself," I say, hoping that the words coming out of my mouth are the right things to say to him.

I'm not a parent, and this is all new to me, but I love this boy as if he were my child, just like I love his mom.

Before I have time to think any further, Brayden lunges out of the car and into my arms. He wraps his arms around my neck, laying his head on my shoulder.

We sit like this for a moment, and for the first time since I got here, I can't imagine a life without this in it - family, love, Brayden, and London. In fact, the thought of it makes me hold onto Brayden tighter.

"I wish you were my dad," he says. His words are so soft I almost miss them. I find myself wishing I could be his dad, too.

My heart clenches tight, and all my words get stuck in my throat. What do I say to him?

He pulls back slowly and smiles. "You're the best, Mr. Jamie. Thank you."

His words hit me hard, and I have to clear my throat to distract myself from the tears threatening to spill out of my eyes. "Anytime, kid. How 'bout we head to the grocery store now?"

"Yea, okay," he says, sitting back in his seat and buckling the seatbelt.

I gently shut the door and take the brief walk around the car to compose myself. I can't begin to explain what just happened or why, and I can't explain how it felt to hear him say he wished I was his dad. It was like nothing I'd ever felt before, and somehow, everything I needed to hear.

I climb into the driver's seat and start the engine. It's a rough start, the engine grumbling loudly and protesting. I've never driven London's car, so I brush it off, hoping the noise isn't anything too important.

I back out onto the quiet neighborhood street and head in the direction towards the outskirts of town. Once outside city limits, I pick up a little more speed. It doesn't take long to get to the grocery store, or so that's what Google Maps says.

I see the large green sign for the store up ahead and put my indicator on to turn. I hit the brake lightly to begin slowing down, only it doesn't work. The car stays at the steady speed of 45 mph.

I tap the brake again, slightly harder this time. Still nothing.

I hit it again, even harder, but the car still doesn't slow down. We speed past the grocery store, and panic sets into my brain.

I slam my foot down on the brake to where the pedal is touching the floor. We're still moving.

Shit. Fuck. Any other curse word I can think of. What the hell do I do?

"Um, Mr. Jamie, the grocery store was back there," Brayden says, concern etched in his voice.

I try to keep my voice as calm and even as possible when I speak. "Yes, I know, B. I didn't see it in time. I'm going to turn around up here."

He mumbles an okay, and I focus once again on the problem at hand.

The brakes clearly went out, but how do I get the car to stop. I'm not a fucking mechanic. I don't know how to do this shit. That's what stunt doubles are for in Hollywood!

Just then, a cyclist signals that they're making a left turn, right in front of me. Fuck, I groan. We're moving too fast, inching closer and closer to the cyclist. He's not going to make it across in time.

So, I swerve hard to the right, narrowly missing him. We fly off the road into a ditch. The front bumper slams into the hard beach-packed soil. My body flies forward and slams back against the weathered cloth seat.

"B, are you okay?" I whisper, feeling the ache in my neck and ribs instantly after impact.

He doesn't respond. I glance back over my shoulder, my body sending a painful protest through my muscles. Brayden's head is back against the seat. His eyes are closed and a large cut frames his forehead. Shit, he must have been looking out the window and smacked his head on it during impact.

I turn back around, trying to unbuckle my seatbelt, but I can't get it to let loose. I jiggle it around, hoping to jimmy it out somehow, but nothing works.

I lean my head against the seat, feeling weaker than usual. I let my eyes close as I fall into blackness.

This cannot be happening again.

Thirty-Five
London

I don't know how long I've been sitting here on the floor bawling my eyes out, but I do know there are no more tears left to cry. I wipe the remnants of the previous ones off my face and stand. I should probably start prepping the vegetables. The boys should be back any minute.

As I dig through the cabinet searching for the cutting board, I hear my phone ringing from the other side of the kitchen. I wander over to the island, laughing quietly to myself. I'm pretty sure it's Jamie calling to make sure he got the right items. I have no doubt he rarely does his own grocery shopping.

It's not Jamie, though. It's a number I don't recognize. I hesitate to pick it up at first but decide I should just in case. It's probably just one of those annoying spam calls.

"Hello," I say, after hitting the green button.

"Hello, is this Ms. McKenzie?" A strange deep voice on the phone asks.

My heart begins to pound harder, and I'm starting to think answering the phone was a bad idea. "Yes," I respond, slightly confused.

"This is Matthew, a nurse at the Low Country Hospital…" he continues explaining that they have my son and need me to come in, but I can barely hear what he's saying over the sound of my heartbeat in my ears.

My stomach churns, and for a moment, I think I might be sick, but I force the bile back down my throat. I can't lose it right now, not when my son needs me.

Jamie.

Oh no, what about Jamie? I don't recall the nurse mentioning anything about him. What does that mean? Is he okay?

Tears that I thought were all dried up spring to my eyes. I try to ask the nurse about him, but no words come out.

"We'll see you soon," the nurse states, and I hang up the phone.

There's no point staying on the call when I can't even speak anyway. I toss my phone into my bag and reach for my keys, only to realize they aren't there.

Damn, how could I forget? Jamie took Brayden to the store in my car.

I dig through my bag, pulling my phone out and dialing the first number to pop up in my contacts.

"Hello," Sabrina's cheery voice does nothing to calm my nerves.

"I need you to come get me right now." Panic fuels the soft growl that comes out in my words.

"I'm on my way," Sabrina states, not even asking what I need and hanging up the phone.

Within a few minutes, I'm climbing into the front seat of Sabrina's tiny sedan. I barely get my seat belt buckled before she pulls out onto the road again.

"Where are we headed?" she asks.

"The hospital." She turns onto Main Street and heads out of town towards Charleston.

She keeps her eyes steady on the road, but I can hear her uneven breathing. "Why are we going to the hospital?" she questions cautiously.

I glance out the window, not wanting to see the sadness in her eyes when I tell her. The buildings pass by quickly as we make our way out of town. I exhale a deep breath, reminding myself that this could be worse.

"Brayden," I finally say.

There's a slight hitch in Sabrina's breathing, and I know she's freaking out. She loves Brayden almost as much as I do. Hell, she's like his second mom, always watching him when I have to work.

"Is he okay?" she mumbles.

"I think so, but honestly, I wasn't listening much after the man on the phone said he was a nurse. I knew it had to be Brayden, and panic just set in." I lean my head against the window, my hand covering my eyes. "As if this day couldn't get any worse."

"What do you mean?"

I lift my head up and look out the front window of the car. We're headed down the interstate now, not too far from the exit for the hospital.

"I saw B's father at the store after work. That's why they were out in the first place. I saw him and lost all rational thought. I forgot half the shit I ran in there for in the first place. I just needed to get away from him as fast as possible. Then, I got home and realized I forgot everything, and Jamie offered to go get them from the store. He took my car and Brayden and and..." I realize I'm rambling. I'm speaking so fast I can't catch my breath.

I try sucking in any amount of air I can, but nothing will come.

Sabrina's hand finds my shoulder. "Okay, you need to calm down. Look, we're turning into the hospital right now. Don't worry about the jackass. Just focus on Brayden." I hear her words, but I don't process them. They don't give me any kind of comfort, not when my mind is whirling with the realization that my ex has ruined my life once again.

Why does every bad thing that happens in my life have something to do with him?

I know he didn't directly cause what happened, but that doesn't stop me from blaming him; if I hadn't seen him, I wouldn't have forgotten anything, and Jamie and Brayden wouldn't have been out.

I grab my chest with my hand, sucking in short breaths that don't give me much oxygen at all. I'm shaking so bad and sweating all over. I've reached full on panic attack mode, and I can't seem to calm myself down.

I do what the counselor taught me years ago. I count to ten. Doesn't work. I tense my muscles and relax them. That doesn't do shit because my muscles are so damn tense they won't relax. I think about everything I'm grateful for, and the first thing that pops into my head is Brayden. My sweet Brayden, and that's when my breathing becomes steadier. I need to get to my son.

Sabrina stops the car in the closest spot to the Emergency Department and turns to me. Both her hands land on one of my shoulders. Her eyes meet mine, and the intensity in them startles me. "You need to calm down. Take a deep breath in." Both she and I suck in a breath. "Now, let it out slowly." I force the air out of my lungs, feeling an almost instantaneous relaxation in my body. "Now, do it again a couple more times."

We both take several more deep breaths together until I'm no longer gasping for air or shaking.

"Good," she whispers. "Let's go check on Brayden."

We climb out of the car and head into Emergency. My mind is much more focused now with Brayden at the center of it. The nurse at the front desk directs us back to his room. I'm so impatient to see my son that my legs move faster than they ever have before. I'm not quite running, but I'm definitely not walking either.

We reach his room in record time, and my heart screams out inside me when it sees my precious baby so tiny and frail against the large hospital bed frame.

I run to him instantly with blinders on. Nothing and no one is going to stop me from getting close to my son.

I finally reach him. My hands find his arms. His eyes are closed, but he still hears me. "Mom?" he asks, weakly.

"Yes, baby, it's me. Mommy's here now. Don't worry," I whisper, tears flooding my cheeks. "I'm right here."

Thirty-Six

Jamie

She doesn't see me sitting off to the side of the room when she walks in, and honestly, I can't blame her. I try to make myself as invisible as possible as she rushes to Brayden, Sabrina not far behind.

Neither of them say anything to me, but Sabrina does give me a sad smile before turning her attention back to Brayden.

I stand slowly, staring at the scene in front of me and letting the guilt eat up my heart.

Once again, I hurt someone. Granted I didn't destroy this family, yet, but I hurt them. I hurt them so deeply, and I can't live with that.

I turn from the room and rush down the hallway and out the double front doors. I can't do this. I can't watch her anguish and know I'm the reason for it.

I told myself I wouldn't let anything like this happen again, and here we are.

I know I didn't do it on purpose, but I hurt the two people I love more than life itself, and they don't even know how I feel about them.

I take in a deep breath as the fresh air hits my body. I begin walking. I don't know where I'm going or how I'm going to get back to Sunrise, but I need to move.

I start in the direction back towards Sunrise and let my legs carry me without thinking.

I let London down. I should have never agreed to this stupid thing in the first place. I knew I'd hurt her if I let it go too far, and that's exactly what happened. I couldn't keep it just sex. No, I had to go and let myself fall for her.

It seems that no matter what I do I always end up hurting the ones around me, the people I love. Sure, we could argue that what happened to them wasn't my fault, and I know that the family in the accident wasn't anyone I knew or loved, but they crossed my path.

I'm the common denominator, the similarity between all of them. Me. No one else.

Clearly, I ruin everything I touch or come in contact with. I shouldn't be allowed near people anymore. I should be put in a cell, locked away, so no one else can get hurt.

Anger, frustration, guilt - they all pulse through my veins, making me clench and unclench my fists with a need to hit or hurt something. But it wouldn't do any good.

I'm a fucking idiot. A dumbass who thought that the promises to never get close to anyone, to never let myself fall in love, were pointless.

I stop walking and look around, realizing I have no clue where I am.

I pull my phone from my pocket and open the Car Lift app on my phone. I rarely ever use this thing because it's not safe to do when you're famous, but I don't have much of a choice at the moment. Besides, I'm the one who led myself into this lion's den.

I search for a car in the area, clicking on the one closest to me.

Five minutes. That's how long I have until the car gets here. That's how long I have to decide if I really want to do this.

It doesn't matter whether I want to do it or not. There is no decision to make. I'm in the middle of nowhere, with no one to come get me.

You have London, the voice in the back of my head screams. I shake it off.

I don't have her. Not after what I did today. I wouldn't be surprised if she never wanted to see me again. Hell, I never want to see myself again, but I know that isn't exactly possible.

She deserves so much more than I can give her, and I'm just a big heaping pile of bad luck. Everything about me screams *stay away*. Why couldn't she see that?

A black sedan pulls up beside me on the side of the road. I don't remember what car was supposed to pick me up, and I don't really give a fuck.

I've decided to put my life in the hands of fate. If something bad happens to me, then so be it. I deserve it.

I swing the back door open and sit down on the soft black leather seats.

"How're you doing this evening, sir?" The gentleman behind the wheel asks, glancing cautiously at me through the rear view.

I suppose that's a good sign. Maybe he's more scared of me than I am of him.

"I've been better," I say, not offering up any more than that.

He pulls out onto the main road, and before I know it, I'm on my way back to Sunrise - the place that was supposed to give me relief from the past and help me find my way back to myself.

It did, you idiot! That same damn voice hollers in my head, but I ignore it.

I found myself alright. I found myself back in the same fucking spot I always do: mourning the loss of someone.

Sure, no one physically died today, but any hopes I had with London sure as hell did.

So much for being happy and forgetting. So much for thinking I was almost back to my old self. So much for thinking I could live a fucking normal life with people I love and getting my own fucking happy ending.

So much for all that shit.

I was naive to think that anything like that would ever happen to me. I may be a fucking movie star, but that doesn't mean a damn thing in the grand scheme of life.

Jamie, bad things happen to people all the time, things we can't control. We have to learn to deal with them, to find the good in them. It's the only way to truly move past them. Think about all the good that's come from what happened. Think about the life you have now. Would you have come to Sunrise if the accident hadn't happened? Would you have met London and Brayden? Would you have understood the real value of love? What happened was a gut-wrenching, life-changing, terrible thing for the family and yourself, but you have to believe there was a purpose for it.

The words from my counselor float through my mind. She'd focused that entire session on finding the good in the bad. I couldn't see how she could turn that accident into something good, not when a family lost their child. She looked at my life, then she looked at that family's life now. She made me examine articles about them, about the things they'd been doing since the accident. One article said they planned to use the money from the lawsuit to fund the music program at the local youth center because they're daughter loved music. Another article talked about their daughter being an organ donor.

My therapist pointed out that we may never understand the

why behind what happens, but we have to find comfort in the good that comes from it. Or we spend our whole lives living in the giant rabbit hole of questions that go unanswered.

Something about that session helps the anger and frustration in me now float away. I don't know what's going to happen from here, but I suppose I can try to find the good in it.

Thirty-Seven
London

I glance around the room for the first time since I walked in. I feel much better knowing that Brayden is okay. The doctor came in a few minutes ago to let me know that all the scans look normal.

Simply knowing that made my heart stop racing and my mind stop wandering to all the bad things that could have happened.

My son is okay. He's alive. He's breathing. And right now, he's chattering on about some TV show he and Jamie were watching before I got home.

Speaking of Jamie, I have no idea where he is. I don't recall seeing him in here when we arrived, but I wasn't exactly looking either. There's no sign that he was even here to begin with.

A soft knock on the door startles me and sends a blink of hope through my body. "Come in," I answer, hoping beyond hope that Jamie opens the door.

I can't help the frown that finds my face when Sabrina walks in with Ki and Hannah following closely behind. Hannah rushes over to Brayden, climbing onto the bed with him and pulling out the toys she brought with her.

"Gee, and we thought you'd be happy to see us," Sabrina mutters, noting the frown on my face.

"You didn't happen to see Jamie when you were wandering through the halls, did you?" I ask, glancing at Brayden and Hannah to make sure they aren't paying us any attention.

Sabrina's brows crease in thought. "No, why? Have you not seen him?"

I shake my head.

"He was here when we arrived, but I haven't seen him since," Sabrina explains.

"Maybe he just stepped out for some fresh air," Ki pipes in with reason.

"Yea, you're probably right." I sigh, hoping he's okay.

"How's B doing?" Ki asks, concern wrinkling her face.

My head turns to him. He's laughing at something Hannah said, and my heart feels so full of something I can't quite explain. "He's better. The doctor said he could go homes in a little bit."

"That's wonderful news," Ki says, pulling me to her side.

"Did they say what happened?" Sabrina questions, coming to the opposite side.

"Car accident. I guess the brakes went out on my Honda and Jamie couldn't get the car to stop. B said there was a guy on a bicycle in the middle of the road and Jamie had to swerve to miss him. They ended up in the ditch just North of the grocery store," I relate the facts as told to me by Brayden and filled in by the nurse.

When Brayden told me what happened, I wasn't even surprised. That old car has seen its better days, and I've known I needed to get some work done on it for a while. I just hadn't realized it was something so important like the damn brakes.

Gah, I feel so guilty for not getting the car checked out and so grateful that Jamie managed to keep my son safe and ignorant from what was happening.

"Oh, wow," both Ki and Sabrina whisper.

"Yea, I can't even imagine how scary that must have been. I'm just so glad they're okay."

"No doubt," Ki agrees.

"What are you going to do about your car?" Sabrina asks thoughtfully.

I haven't even thought about the car until this conversation. I'm sure it's totaled. It was older than dirt, but I'm not even concerned about the car or replacing it. I'm more concerned about finding Jamie and making sure he's okay now that I know Brayden is good.

Something tells me that Jamie is not anywhere near fine. I know his secret. I know what happened with that girl. And I have no doubt that he's currently blaming himself for this accident.

I also know that's why he's disappeared. He's probably on his way back to California right now. As much as I understand what he's dealing with, I'm also furious.

Does he really have that little faith in me that he'd think I'd be upset or mad at him? Does he have no feelings for us?

He must not since it was so easy for him to just walk away from us when we needed him most, when *I* needed him most.

And I do need him. So much, right now. I need my person here to lean on.

Don't get me wrong, my best friends are amazing, but it's not the same. They're not the ones I want comforting me right now or sharing this experience with me.

"Ya know, I don't know," I finally answer. "I'm more worried about Jamie than I am the damn car at this point."

Ki smiles like she wants to say "I told you so" and looks directly at me. "I," she begins, but I cut her off.

"I know what you're going to say, but please don't. Yes, you were right I do love him. Probably more than I should for only knowing him for such a short time. But I'm not sure it even matters anymore."

Her face drops into a frown. "What do you mean you're not sure it matters anymore?"

"What she said!" Sabrina butts in.

I roll my eyes and sigh. "Come on guys, he's not even here. I know he left. No one has seen him since we arrived. What kind of man does that - just walks away from the woman who needs him?"

"You don't know why he left," Ki insists.

"Yea," Sabrina agrees. "He could have left to go get you food or to take a shit?"

I glare at her. "Really?"

She shrugs her shoulders. "What? Some people don't like taking a shit in public places."

"By some people, you mean yourself," Ki says.

"I'm not ashamed to admit it," Sabrina mutters.

"Okay, whatever, it doesn't matter," I say, bringing them back to the point of the conversation. "The point is I don't think he feels the same way about me, so what's the point in trying to find him and checking on him?"

"What's the point?" Sabrina asks, flabbergasted. "Are you kidding me?"

Ki smacks her playfully. "Stop being so dramatic." Then, she looks at me. "You love him. That's the point."

"But he doesn't love me," I whine almost like a child, and I hate how I'm acting.

"Has he told you that?"

"No."

"Then how do you know?" Ki asks, rationally.

She really needs to stop this whole being rational thing. I remember mere months ago when she was the least rational and mature person I knew. Now, here she is being all "you don't know he doesn't love you because you haven't asked him" and shit.

I fold my arms in front of my chest, pouting slightly.

"Look, he'd be crazy not to love you. Maybe he's scared that you don't love him, and you'll hate him for hurting your son. Hell, there could be a thousand other reasons, but you won't know for sure until you talk to him."

I hate it when she's right.

Thirty-Eight

Jamie

After my revelation and the driver dropped me off at the hotel, I found myself too anxious and upset to go up to my room. Instead, I made my way out the back of the hotel and down to the beach, where I'm walking now.

Tiny crabs rush across the sand, avoiding my feet the best they can. The remnants of the sunset create a thin line of pinks and golds behind the hotel, while the moonlight makes its ascent over the horizon on the ocean.

The water is calm tonight, waves sloshing softly in the warm coastal breeze. I suck in the deep scent of salt and seaweed as I continue my way north on the beach.

My phone thumps against my leg as I walk, begging me to pull it out and call London, to check on Brayden, but I resist the urge. I'm not sure I'm ready to face her just yet. I'm not ready to hear what she has to say, and I know she'll be pissed.

If she isn't upset about the accident, she'll damn sure be upset about the fact I left the hospital when she wasn't looking and wasn't there by her side. I know her well enough to know that much. She may be able to forgive me for both accidents but walking out on her when she needed me most, that I'm not so sure about.

A soft buzz vibrates against my leg, and I slip my phone out, careful not to drop it in the waves currently surrounding my feet.

"Hello," I mumble, the roar of the waves diminishing my voice even more.

"Hey," Damon's voice sounds across the phone. Even from thousands of miles away, he still seems to know when I need him most.

"I fucked it all up," I admit, running my free hand across my chest as the persistent ache reminds me I'm still alive.

"What are you talking about?"

I suck in a deep breath and stare out in front of me at the darkening sea. "I was driving and --"

"Wait, you were driving?" Damon cuts me off. "That's great, man. You haven't driven since the accident." The excitement in his voice damn near kills me.

"No, it's not great," I bite out hard and angry. "The brake's stopped working and I crashed into a ditch, with London's son in the car."

Silence fills Damon's end of the line except for bits of static. I can only imagine what he's thinking - if the press gets a hold of this, they'll have a field day.

"Is he okay? Are you okay?" His questions surprise me. I expected him to start talking about how this is going to mess up my reputation even more, but he doesn't.

"Yea, he's fine. I'm fine, physically anyway."

"Shit, Jamie, I'm sorry this happened, but I'm glad everyone's okay."

"Yea, me too. I'm just not sure London and I will be okay after this," I say, rubbing my eyes with my free hand.

"For your sake, I hope you are, but that's actually got a little bit to do with why I was calling you," Damon says, changing the subject. I'm sure he has no idea what to say to me since relationships and him don't mix well. As far as I know, he's never been in love, not once.

"How so?" I sigh.

"Well, I got a call today from a producer on a new superhero movie. They want you to play the main character, Satar or something like that. Anyways, they think you'd be perfect for the part, and they want you in LA tomorrow for an audition and chemistry read with your costar."

My gut clenches tight. The ache in my chest worsens. And an image of London pops into my mind. "Tell them I pass," I say, without thinking.

I can't go back to that life, and more importantly, I don't want to. I have a life here, a family. At least, I hope I still do. Even if I don't, I need to be here to find that out. If I thought London would be pissed because I left the hospital, I can only imagine how angry she'd be if I left Sunrise without talking it all through with her.

I don't need to talk it through with her, though, because I know what I want. I want her. I want Brayden. I want to stay in Sunrise.

"Did I hear you correctly?" Damon scoffs.

"Yes, you did. I love you, man, and you've been a great friend and agent, but I'm done. I'm done making movies. I'm done with that life."

"You're sure?"

"Yes," I insist.

It doesn't take much longer for Damon to come up with an excuse to end the call, and honestly, I'm glad. I walk a few feet away from the water and plop down in the dry sand.

Staring out over the ocean, I can see everything I want in my life, in my future. I see London and Brayden, playing in the front yard. I see a little baby girl, bouncing excitedly in London's arms. I see barbecues, birthday parties, and Christmases. I see it all with my family.

Because that's what they are.

They're my family. I don't know how I found them, and I don't care. All I know is that I don't want to live this life without them, and if that means I have to fight for them, I will fight with everything I have. I'll make London see that I'm serious, that she's all I ever wanted. And she'll know how sorry I am that I left her when she needed me most. She'll know I'll never do it again.

But most importantly, she'll know how much she and Brayden mean to me and how much I love them.

Thirty-Nine
London

"Hey, B," I whisper, sitting on the edge of his bed and brushing his hair off his forehead. "Aunt Sabrina is going to stay here with you for a bit while I go out. Is that okay?"

"Yea." He nods. "Are you going to find Jamie?"

I snap my eyes to his face. "Why do you ask, bud?"

"I heard you talking at the hospital about how he left. Mom, I don't want him to go. You have to find him and bring him back." The sadness in his voice slices my heart open.

"Awe, honey, I don't know if I'll be able to bring him back, but I'll try," I say, my eyes filled with unshed tears.

"You have to, Mama," he mutters softly before sleep takes over. I rub my thumb across his forehead and down his cheek, kissing him softly.

I study my son's pale face and the gash that took seven stitches to close it up. I knew this would be hard, the day when Jamie would disappear, but I didn't realize just how hard it would be.

I stand, walking out of the room and down the stairs to the living room where Sabrina sits on the couch. She turns towards me as I reach the bottom step. "How's he doing?"

"I think he's okay now, just tired." I answer, sitting down next to her on the couch.

"And how are you doing?" she asks.

I lean my head back against the soft microfiber cushion, closing my eyes. The reality of everything that happened today comes crashing back - Hamish, the accident, the hospital, Jamie. Tears slide from my eyes as I cover my face with my hands.

"I'm a mess," I mutter through the tears.

Sabrina gently tugs me to her, wrapping me up in a sisterly hug. Sobs catch in my throat as I try to speak. "Why? Why me?"

"Oh, honey," Sabrina coos, rubbing her hands up and down my arms and trying to comfort me.

I continue to cry until I can't cry anymore. A soft hiccup escapes from my lips. "I love him, Sabrina. He protected my boy, then he left. He left me alone to face all this. What do I do with that?"

"I think you know exactly what you need to do with that. You need to go see him and demand some answers because you deserve them." She makes it sound so simple, so easy, like it should be common sense.

But why should I go after a man who left me, who walked away when I needed him? I know there are a thousand reasons why he could have left, but do any of them justify the action?

The weight of today sits on my shoulders, and I recall the conversation we had not too long ago when Jamie said that maybe we weren't meant to carry everything on our own. If he meant what he said, then why did he leave me to deal with *this* on my own?

"Why should I be the one to go after him? Shouldn't he be coming to me, begging me to forgive him?"

Sabrina shrugs her shoulders. "I don't know, should he? Maybe that's how they did it back in the days when women had no say in their lives, but I'm not sure that's how it has to be today. Honey, you're a strong, independent woman who knows what she wants. Why do you need to wait for the man to come get you? Why can't you go get him?"

"Because I wasn't the one to walk away," I mumble, stubborn as always.

"No, but if you sit here and don't do anything, then you will be. Is that how you really want this to go?"

I don't know. Is it? Could I accept if I decide to wait for Jamie to show up and he never does? Could I live with knowing I didn't do everything I could to keep the man I love in my life?

I'm not sure I could, but I'm also not sure I can face him. What if he doesn't want me like I thought he did? What if that's why he left? What if he realized that I'm not worth it like Hamish did?

Could I live with showing up at his hotel room only to find out that he doesn't want me?

Sabrina puts her hands on both my cheeks, turning my face to meet hers. "I know what Hamish did to you hurt you, and I know that Jamie not being there at the hospital for you brought back those feelings, but if you really love Jamie like you say you do, then you need to fight for him. I can almost guarantee that he's probably fighting the same internal battle you are, and if neither of you gives in, then you're both screwed. So be the woman that I know you are, get off this damn couch, and go get your man."

Her words light a fire under my butt, and I push myself off the couch. She's right. I can be scared, and I can let what Hamish did destroy this relationship, or I can fight for what I want.

And I want Jamie. So, what choice do I have but to fight?

Forty
Jamie

After I don't know how long of staring out over the ocean, I stand, making my way back up to the hotel. I know what I want. For the first time in I can't remember, I actually know what I want. The excitement threatens to bust out of me as I head towards the elevator and back to my room.

First, I intend to take a shower and wash this dreadful day off me. Then, I intend to go to London's house and apologize for everything I've done and everything I've put her through.

When I finally make it to my floor, I step off the elevator and walk down the hall to my room. I slide the key card in the door and open it. I stop mid-step into the room.

There's a light on in the small living area of the suite. Did I walk into the wrong room? I glance back, checking the number on the door. Nope, this is the right room.

I quietly sneak into the room, planning to creep up on whoever is in here, but they don't give me the chance.

"Jamie, thank God," the voice that's recently become like home to me sounds through the room, sending chills down my back.

"London?" I ask as she comes into view. Her small frame sits cross-legged in the middle of the couch, a single light by the TV shining on her face. "What are you doing here? Why aren't you at the hospital?"

"I could ask you the same thing." Her voice is hard as she eyes me angrily.

"I didn't think you'd want me there," I admit, looking down at the carpeted floor beneath my feet. I don't want to look at her. I don't want to see the disappointment bound to be showing in her eyes.

She stands up abruptly, walking towards me and stopping just in front of me. "How could you possibly think that?"

"I hurt you," I say, not knowing how else to explain my decision.

"Yea." She nods. "You did hurt me."

"Exactly." I move away from her towards the bed on the other side of the room.

Her eyes follow me as I make the distance between us larger. I stare into their blue depths, seeing nothing but sadness floating within them and gutting me to the core.

"You hurt me because you weren't there. You *left* Jamie. Why'd you leave?" she pleads with me to be honest, to tell her the painful truth.

"I did what I always do. I hurt the ones I love. I couldn't stand watching you stare at Brayden in that bed. I couldn't stand what I'd done to you, to him."

"What do you mean what you've done? Did you cut the brake line?"

I shake my head. "Of course not."

"Did you do everything you could to fix the problem?"

I nod my head vigorously, not sure where she's going with this conversation.

"Did you try to protect my son?"

"You know I did," I say, agony in my voice.

"Then, why do you think this is your fault?"

"Because everyone connected to me dies or gets hurt," I yell at her. My voice is so loud and harsh that I don't even recognize it, and I hate how it sounds. I see the pain growing deeper in her eyes. I know I'm hurting her, but I don't know how to stop it.

She shakes her head slowly as she walks towards me. "Is that what you really think? That you're the problem?"

"Aren't I?" I ask, tears filling my eyes.

What is it about this woman that always makes me feel so

vulnerable, so seen, so - so loved?

She reaches me and stops merely inches away from me. She's so much shorter than I am, I have to look down to see her face. She places her hands on my chest and turns her eyes up to me.

"You," she states firmly, "are not the problem. In fact, for me, you're the solution. You taught me that it's okay to go all in, even when everything is so completely unsure. You taught me that it's good to go after what I want, that I deserve that much. There isn't a damn thing I would change about you."

Her words pierce my icy heart, melting what was left of the protective shield I'd placed around it.

She points her finger at my chest and stares me down. "You are the best thing to ever happen to me. Do you understand that?"

I nod my head. It's the only thing I can do. I fully expected her to come here, feisty and fuming at the fact I hurt her son, but I never, in a million years, saw this coming.

"And you're a damn fool if you don't know I love you with everything I have," she whispers. Her voice is so soft I almost miss it.

My lips turn into a small smile and my arms wrap around her, pulling her tight against me. "I love you, too," I declare - no regret, no shame.

I feel her soft lips twisting up into a smile against my chest. "You do?" she mumbles against me.

"More than I ever expected," I admit.

She pushes against my tight grip so she can see me again. A

naughty smile forms on her lips. "Oh, I'm well aware of what you intended." She winks at me.

I can't help but laugh, then Brayden pops in my mind. "How is he? Is he okay?"

"Yea, he's fine," she smiles. "Actually, he's at home with Sabrina, and he was asking where you were. Wanted me to find you and bring you back. He loves you, ya know?"

Her words hit me in the deepest part of my soul, and tears fill my eyes. "I love him, too. I'm so sorry I wasn't there for him or you. I got scared. I needed to be anywhere but there."

She lays her hand on my chest, smoothing out a wrinkle in my shirt. "It's okay. I get it. Just don't ever do it again," she whispers, and I can't contain myself any longer.

"Fuck, I love you," I growl, claiming her lips with mine. Our lips connect in a greedy fashion. It might have only been a few hours where I thought I'd lost her, but it felt like a lifetime.

Need grows within me. I reach my hands under her ass and grab on tight as I lift her up, carrying her to the king size bed only feet away.

I set her down gently, our lips still fighting and raging with each other. We're so close I can barely breathe, and yet, it feels like I need her even closer.

I break my lips from hers. "Lay down," I demand.

I expect her to run off at the mouth with protests, but she surprises me by doing exactly as I say. I unbutton her blouse while I run kisses up and down her neck. Pulling the blouse away from her, I trail kisses down her stomach.

She situates herself around me, tossing her shirt to the side and somehow managing to unclasp her bra without ruining my fun.

When my lips reach the hem of her dress pants, my hands find the button, pulling them down until they're merely a puddle on the floor at my feet.

I study her - my love - laying in front of me, open and waiting for me to claim her as mine both verbally and physically. And that's exactly what I intend to do. Tonight, and every night for the rest of our lives.

Epilogue - 1 year and 2 months later
London

I glance around the living room, decked out in garland, lights, and country Christmas signs. In the corner, just beside the TV our large and very fake Christmas tree stands, an odd assortment of homemade ornaments covering it from head to toe.

My mom would cringe if she could see our tree and its homemade adornments. She always believed that everything about Christmas should be perfectly put together, but not me, I rather enjoy the ornaments Brayden and I make for the tree each year.

I hold the warm mug of hot cocoa close to my chest. An arm snakes around my waist, and Jamie kisses my neck.

"What are you still doing up?" he whispers close to my ear, sending shivers through me.

After the night of the accident, Jamie and I sat down and had a real talk about everything we wanted. He told me he was giving up his career and that he wanted to stay here with me. I told him I couldn't think of anything I wanted more. Then, we talked to B. We told him about us, about our plans, and he jumped with joy at Jamie becoming part of our lives for good.

A few months later, Jamie moved in with us, and a few months after that, he proposed. And, two months ago on the one year anniversary of that day, we got married. Something about celebrating our love on the day we finally confessed it to each other just made sense.

But those things aren't the reason I'm still awake. Not even close.

"Just can't sleep," I respond softly.

He wraps his other arm around me and pulls me in tight to his chest. "Wouldn't have anything to do with the Christmas present we have for Brayden tomorrow, would it?"

I smile. "Maybe."

I've honestly never been so excited to give him a present like I am now. It's the one thing I always wished I could give him but didn't know how to. And it's something Jamie brought up long before I ever thought of it.

"Are you worried he won't be happy with it?" He asks, his

insecurity clear in his voice.

"No," I assure him. I'm not worried about it at all. I know Brayden will love his present.

He lets out a breath. "Good, because I really want him to like it."

I turn around in his arms, so I'm facing him. "He loves you more than anything in this world. This gift you're giving him will make him happier than anything ever could."

He leans down, his lips meeting my forehead. "I so hope you're right. Come on, let's get to bed before it's too late."

Jamie

I've never been so nervous in my life. I wasn't even this nervous when I proposed to London or on our wedding day. No, I've never felt anything like this. I'm sweating everywhere. My pulse is racing. And I'm so antsy that sitting down doesn't even seem possible.

That's why I'm pacing behind the couch right now as Brayden opens his presents. He's opening up some remote-control car he wanted at the moment, but there's one present left. One small, rectangular present still waiting for him to rip it open, and the anticipation might just be the death of me.

London glances over the back of the couch at me. "Jamie, calm down. It's going to be okay."

I shake my head. I'm not so sure. This is a huge step for me, and I'm terrified of what Brayden will think about it.

He lays the car off to the side and reaches for the last present. "Last one," he squeals excitedly. He turns it in his hands, shakes it, and holds it close to his ear, trying to guess what it is.

"B, just open it, then you'll know what it is," London instructs.

He rolls his eyes, then rips into the paper. When all the paper is off, a small white box sits in his hands. He flips the lid open and looks at the papers inside. His eyes widen as I picture the words he's staring at right now - Petition for Adoption.

He looks at London, then to me and back to London. "Did you read what it says?" she asks.

He nods his head. "And what do you think?"

He drops the box with the papers and runs around the couch to me, wrapping his arms around my waist. "You're going to be my dad, for real?"

"Yea, bud. I'm going to be your dad. Are you okay with that?"

He looks up at me, his eyes red from tears. "This is the best Christmas ever," he yells, hugging me tighter.

I wrap my hand around his head, and I can't help the tears now streaming down my face. "For me too, kid."

I turn my head to London who's still sitting on the couch, tears twinkling in her eyes. "I love you," I mouth to her.

"I love you, too," she mouths back.

And I know that everything I've been through led me to this moment.

Acknowledgements

I don't know why writing this page is always so hard for me because I'm constantly saying thank you to everyone for everything. But for some reason, I can't seem to decide whom I should thank first. So, in no particular order, here it goes!

First and foremost, thank you to my family. You all are the reason I have the strength and the courage to fight for my dreams, to make every single one of them come true. For the longest time, I felt unlovable and completely broken, but you're always there to remind me that I'm worthy of all the love and gifts this world has to offer.

Thank you to my wonderful and talented husband. Not only have you supported me on this journey in every way possible, but you've also covered all my design and layout needs. You are truly a blessing, and our love inspires my stories every day.

Thank you to the absolutely amazing Bethany Hendrix for taking time out of her busy schedule to edit and answer all my pain in the butt questions.

Also, I need to send a shoutout to the incredible Nouna Anthony for redesigning my website and my marketing plan and always believing in my writing, even though she hates reading romance novels.

Of course, I can't forget the wonderful writers, friends, and bloggers that I've met along this journey. You truly are the most amazing and supportive people. I've loved every minute of getting to know you all, and I can't express how much I appreciate you letting me bombard you with questions and promos. Thank you all so much!

And, I desperately need to thank my readers. None of this would be possible without you and your encouragement. I'm beyond grateful for all of you.

Last but not least, I want to thank the good Lord above for giving me the strength I need to keep going each day. My life has not once been easy, but I know I'll make it through.

About the Author

Loran Adelle Davis writes sweet, contemporary romance stories with strong, sassy Southern women as her main characters, and don't let the "sweet" fool you!

She found her love for reading and writing strong female leads while completing her Bachelor's in English at a small Appalachian College. She furthered her craft of writing through her English degree and learned a lot about the stories she wanted to tell the world. With the help of her mentor, the Chair of the English Department, she determined that she would do what she loves – writing.

Currently, she resides in South Carolina. She works on her writing and her business LA Davis Books in the mornings and teaches toddlers in the afternoon. Her love for children and writing hold equal places in her heart. When she isn't writing or working, she enjoys traveling, trying new foods, reading, spending time with her family, and watching Hallmark movies.

Find Me On…

Facebook: www.facebook.com/ladavisbooks

www.facebook.com/loranadelledavis

https://www.facebook.com/groups/loransbooklovers

Instagram: www.instagram.com/loranadelledavis

Twitter: https://twitter.com/LoranDavis

Or Visit My Website

Website: www.ladavisbooks.com

Don't forget to sign up for my newsletter or join my Facebook Reader Group for special updates!

www.ingramcontent.com/pod-product-compliance
Lightning Source LLC
Chambersburg PA
CBHW060534180626
46817CB00002B/573